Darkness Bound

By Lorienne Walk

Writers Exchange E-Publishing

http://www.writers-exchange.com

Darkness Bound

Copyright 2008, 2015, 2023 Lorienne Walk

Writers Exchange E-Publishing

PO Box 372

ATHERTON QLD 4883

Cover Art by: Odile Stamanne

Book flourishes from https://www.freepik.com

Published by Writers Exchange E-Publishing

http://www.writers-exchange.com

The unauthorized reproduction or distribution of this copyrighted work is illegal. Criminal copyright infringement, including infringement without monetary gain, is investigated by the FBI and is punishable by up to 5 (five) years in federal prison and a fine of $250,000.

Names, characters and incidents depicted in this book are products of the author's imagination and are used fictitiously. Any resemblance to actual events, locales, organizations, or persons, living or dead, is entirely coincidental and beyond the intent of the author.

No part of this book may be reproduced or transmitted in any form or any means, electronic or mechanical, including photocopying, recording, or by any information storage and retrieval system, without permission from the publisher.

Contents

Chapter 1

Chapter 2

Chapter 3

Chapter 4

Chapter 5

Chapter 6

Chapter 7

Chapter 8

Chapter 9

Chapter 10

About the Author

Heart's Desires and Dark Embraces_By Margaret L. Carter

Mischief in Moonstone Series_By Christine DeSmet

Nitesh_By JennaKay Francis

Passion in the Blood_By Margaret L. Carter

Sealing the Dark Portal_By Margaret L. Carter

Shadow of the Beast_By Margaret L. Carter

Sweet Dreams_By Karen Wiesner

The Faery Sickness_By JennaKay Francis

Woodcutter's Grim Series

Chapter 1

She would get the letter today.

"Happy birthday, Sarah. You've talked yourself out of a good time again." Sarah Berkley stared at herself in the mirror of the ladies' restroom and tried to work up some emotion. It was her twenty-fourth birthday, and she'd just shot down, figuratively speaking, the only proposition she was likely to receive all night. For some reason, this didn't bother her.

It wasn't as if Mark had been impolite. On the contrary, he'd acted quite the gentleman, but Sarah could see, as if in a crystal ball, the short future of any relationship they tried to build. And as for a one-night-stand--she had dismissed the thought immediately. That reeked of desperation, and Sarah wasn't desperate. Being desperate implied that you cared.

A faded girl living a faded life, she thought. Her reflection agreed with her. It was a reflection of a tall, pale woman with long blonde hair. Even her eyes were a pale blue, and they gazed dispassionately at the world, although those who cared to look saw a hint of steel in them.

She supposed she should go back out there; her friends would be wondering what was keeping her otherwise. She thought about their lively conversation and about having to cross the crowded dance floor again and sighed. She'd been feeling tired and jaded lately; nothing seemed really interesting any more. Maybe it was just a bout of birthday blues, but it was a really strong one.

Maybe she'd go to the range tomorrow. The thought of standing in one spot for two hours and unloading a box and a half of ammunition into some cardboard was the only thing that interested her much nowadays. She was getting good, too. A ghost of a smile flitted across her face as she contemplated her chances of winning next month's competition.

She was quite sure Mark wouldn't understand that. With something of a shock, she realized that she'd been subconsciously categorizing everyone into two groups--the normal people, and her. It sounded so arrogant when she thought about it that way, but it was the truth. So what was she waiting for? Someone *abnormal?* Someone like her? *Keep dreaming,* she told herself. *Relationships with other people involved compromise.* No wonder she was so mediocre at it.

"Sarah! There you are. Are you all right? That guy didn't try anything weird, did he?" Rebecca also worked for Sarah's company, and it was she who'd pushed the hardest for this outing.

"Oh, no, he didn't try anything." Sarah looked back from the mirror. "I just told him 'thanks but no thanks'."

"But *why*, Sarah? He seemed like a nice man to me. You're too picky; it's not like you're going to marry him. Just have a little fun."

Sarah just sighed, and Rebecca gave her a look that plainly said she thought Sarah had forgotten the meaning of the word.

"Girl, you have to try and loosen up a bit. You look like you're going to just up and fade away someday. Try living a bit."

"I am living," Sarah said defensively and then she plastered on what she hoped was a reassuring smile. "I'm sorry, Becky. I guess I'm just feeling down about today. Getting old and stuff, you know?"

"You're too young to do that." Rebecca rolled her eyes, but she didn't press the subject. "Let's just get back out there. Maybe you'll find someone you don't even know you're looking for."

Sarah didn't think she'd find someone like that in a place like this. *Where would I find someone like that?* she wondered. Her reflection gazed back cynically at her. Transylvania maybe; with her pale complexion and blank expression she thought she looked like a bloody vampire.

To the surprise of no one, Sarah went home alone. Rebecca had proposed they try somewhere else, but she'd caught the look in Sarah's eye and hadn't repeated the suggestion.

Sarah unlocked the door to her apartment and flicked on the light. She'd been living there for over a year, but the walls were still bare; she didn't care much about interior decoration. Or exterior decoration, if it came to that.

She stooped and scooped up a pile of mail. Bills and birthday greetings made up the bulk of the letters. She was sure her foster parents had sent her more money, as if she was still in college. She kicked off her heels and with a sigh of relief plopped onto the couch.

She started sorting her mail, throwing junk at the wastepaper basket. She stopped when she came to an official looking envelope from a law firm by the name of Sawyer and Moore. The name rang a tiny bell in Sarah's head. She had heard of this firm before, but she couldn't recall where. She put the other letters aside and tore open the envelope.

She scanned the missive inside and felt her eyes widen with shock. The letter was written in the language of lawyers, just close enough to English to be comprehensible. Sarah comprehended. She comprehended all too well.

"Inheritance," she murmured, the word conjuring up images of crowns and thrones and ties by blood. Sarah felt a cold serpent of fear start to uncoil in her stomach. Her real parents. Her real past.

Sarah dropped the letter and headed for the kitchen to pour herself a generous measure of something, anything, floor polish if need be. She stopped and gently closed the cupboard door.

"No. Gotta keep my wits about me." She was aware that she wasn't acting rationally, but she had to do something. Had to keep calm. She did all the washing up, and her ironing, and was halfway through vacuuming the floors when she felt tired enough to go to sleep.

She tumbled into bed, sheer exhaustion pulling her eyes closed. Suddenly she sat up again, went over to the safe, took out one of her pistols, loaded it, and placed it on the stand beside her bed. *If I'm going to be paranoid*, she thought, *I might as well go the whole way.*

She'll contact the lawyers on Monday. Tuesday at the latest. She has to wonder what she's inherited.

It hadn't been an unpleasant weekend. Sarah hadn't given it a chance to be. She was at the range by nine in the morning, and stayed there until the last of the other shooters packed up after dark. She went back home reeking of gunpowder and oil and sweat. Her arms ached, and she knew she was probably messing up her chances for the competition, but sanity, she decided, was more important than another trophy.

She was in control, she decided, and she was handling it. She was handling it her own way, on her own terms. It was perfectly normal to be a bit anxious about a past one couldn't remember. And the nightmares were enough to frighten anyone.

She was twelve years old again. She was on her hands and knees, cold flagstones under her fingers. She could feel warm blood flowing from a gaping wound in her leg. She pulled herself to her feet. She had to run. All her pursuers had to do was follow the trail of her blood. She stumbled on in the darkness.

Her questing fingers found an iron door. Pale, shaking hands struggled with the locks and bolts. Behind the door something waited. She could feel it. It was merely existing; dead, but still dreaming. The twenty-four year old Sarah screamed inside the young Sarah's head, begging her not to undo those last few locks. The girl didn't hear her. Dizzy with lack of blood, the girl pushed on the door, falling into the darkness within.

Sarah woke with a scream and grabbed blindly for her Margolin semi-automatic. Drenched in sweat, she held the gun in trembling fingers, like a child would hold a favorite toy. Eventually she placed the gun back on the bedside table and buried her face in her hands. *Why are they coming back now?* she wondered despairingly. She knew of course. The answer lay in a letter still lying where it had fallen three days ago.

She had a scalding hot shower and scrubbed at her face, trying to erase the memories of her dreams. *I'll sell it all,* she told herself. *I'll get rid of everything they've left me. I'll auction it, or even pay someone to junk it. Nothing can be worse than this.*

Her courage fortified by these resolutions, she forced herself to eat a tasteless breakfast in front of her web browser and then picked up the phone. *There's no sense procrastinating,* she decided, *the sooner I get this over and done with the sooner life can go back to normal.*

She has to come here. The lawyers will want her to sign things in person. She'll need a couple days to pack, of course. She'll be here in a week, at the most. She'll come, she must.

The Sawyer and Moore law firm was tucked away discreetly between an ophthalmologist's surgery and a small café in a part of town that had been politely decaying for the best part of twenty years. In fact, Sarah felt the entire town was slowly crumbling back into the rolling countryside.

With the detachment of someone who had learnt it in a book, she knew she had grown up around Armstead. To her relief, although some of the buildings and thoroughfares seemed vaguely familiar, nothing in the dozing town woke the fear that slumbered uneasily in her mind.

The trip up had been relatively pleasant. Sarah wanted to spend as little time as possible in Armstead, but had sensibly packed enough for a couple weeks, or longer if the need arose. She had also taken the better part of her firearms collection. She felt a bit silly, giving in to her paranoia like that, but decided it was better to feel silly than frightened.

As she had traveled farther north, the countryside grew darker and lusher. Small farms and forests broke the monotony of the rolling hills, and she wound down the windows to better enjoy the clean country air. *There's nothing to be afraid of,* she told herself cheerfully, as she hummed along to her collection of sixties classics. *It was just the trauma of losing my parents so young,* she recited the therapist's words in her head like a mantra. Just an overactive imagination, he'd said, although Sarah was bright enough to know that her case had puzzled him.

Although she knew no one, she was waved to several times as she motored along the quiet streets of Armstead. She supposed that tourists were a rarity here, and she smiled and waved back. A young man on a bicycle loaded up with groceries directed her to the town's only law firm. She smiled and thanked him, and drove on.

"Welcome back, Ms Berkley," he called cheerfully after her. Sarah felt her face grow cold. They *did* know her after all. They recognised her after all these years, welcomed her back as if she'd only been away a week. Her first instinct was to put the car in gear and drive as far and as fast as she could away from this place. She took deep breaths, recited the therapist's words again and drove on.

Moore reminded Sarah of a turtle. His long, thin neck supported a nearly bald head that craned forward to peer at her short-sightedly. He courteously got up from behind his polished wooden desk and shook Sarah's hand before directing her to a chair.

"Welcome back, Miss Berkley. Armstead has missed your family's presence."

"I'm not planning on staying," Sarah replied quickly. "I just want to get these affairs in order."

"I see." Moore sounded vaguely disappointed, but his professional manner soon reasserted itself. "The terms of your father's will were rather unusual. That is to be expected of course. Your father was a great man."

"I don't remember him," Sarah replied tonelessly. This wasn't quite the truth, as she had one fragment of a memory. A large, warm hand holding hers as she stood in front of a grave festooned with flowers, and a voice in her ear, telling her she would be protected. She flung the useless memory away, and concentrated on Moore's reading.

"All assets to be held in trust until the occasion of my daughter's twenty-fourth birthday." Moore paused and looked up at her, to make sure she was listening. "At this time I assume she will have completed her education, without yet being bound by the responsibilities of adult life."

"What does *that* mean?" Sarah asked.

"Your father, I assume, expected you to take over the running of the family estate."

"You said assets. What exactly have I inherited?"

"Let me see," he shuffled through some papers, "I'll just give you a general overview, you can peruse the particulars at your leisure. You've inherited the family home and grounds, there's no evaluation, and no expectation that you should sell. Stocks and bonds worth roughly seven million dollars, a collection of bank accounts, total assets around three million dollars, and various antiques and curios currently in storage at the estate worth over twelve million dollars at last evaluation." Moore looked up at her enquiringly.

Sarah's fear had receded in the face of a wave of pure greed. Her mind was trying to wrap itself around the numbers and failing. "I had no idea," she breathed.

"We can recommend an accountant, although I'd imagine you'd prefer one closer to your home. There is some administrative business, of course. I assume you'll want to visit the house." That snapped her out of her dreams of pina coladas and palm trees like a slap in the face. The family home. Again, she had no memories of it, but she knew with visceral certainty that somewhere within its walls was a stone-flagged floor and an iron door.

Where is she? She should be here by now. She must visit, she has to visit. Sarah, where are you? Sarah, please. This is your home.

Sarah stayed in a little bed and breakfast place near the local school. It was clean, if not overly comfortable and the kitchen turned out huge home-cooked meals. She had been here two days. She was now a wealthy woman. She could leave any time, begin a new life. She didn't.

Sarah carefully removed the fat from her bacon. She was eating well here, and enjoying it, but there was no need to go overboard.

She knew what she had to do. Looking out through the lace curtains that adorned practically every window of the little hotel, she could see where the Berkley estate, *her* estate began. It squatted on a hill northeast of Armstead like a mossy gargoyle. Her family obviously hadn't been farmers, for the lands had been left to run wild. Tall, dark trees hid any buildings from view, and a high, if crumbling, stone wall deterred sightseers. As she watched, a murder of crows alighted in one of the towering pines.

She had been informed that her father had arranged for the sprawling mansion to be maintained in the family's absence, and she resolved to visit the housekeeper. It would delay the inevitable moment when she approached the house itself, at least for a few hours.

Sarah felt distinctly uncomfortable being fawned over. The housekeeper and her husband, who occasionally trimmed the weeds around the house, were practically licking her sensible leather shoes. They informed her that they had worked tirelessly to keep the house, *her* house, in pristine condition for her return, and wasn't it wonderful that Berkley Manor had a mistress again. Mrs Cox explained carefully that she hadn't been given the keys to much of the manor, and she was dreadfully sorry, but she just didn't know *what* kind of condition some of the rooms would be in after all these years, but it was wonderful to have you back, dear. To Sarah's relief, it appeared that there was electricity connected, although Mr Cox butted in apologetically to say that it wasn't the most reliable of connections, but with a bit of capital he could fix that right up, yes ma'am. Sarah plastered on a fake grin and made her escape.

It wasn't until she had driven half-way up the hill that she realised where she was going; such was her relief to be away from the sycophantic pair. With an effort of will she calmed herself, and nosed her station wagon through the wrought iron gates.

She's here!

Sarah put the station wagon into first as she eased the car over cobblestones pushed up and broken by tree roots. She winced as she heard something scrape. In amongst the trees the temperature had dropped dramatically, and Sarah stopped briefly to pull on a jacket. The sun had retreated behind a blanket of featureless grey cloud that conspired to add to the dreamlike atmosphere.

After about half a mile of forested wilds Sarah came to another pair of wrought iron gates. The cobbles stopped and she glanced at the enormous ruts and potholes ahead of her with trepidation. She decided this was definitely *not* a place to get stuck, and with some regret she abandoned her vehicle.

As she stepped out of the car the dark trees rustled, as if whispering among themselves, passing on the news that the master was home. Sarah pulled her jacket tighter around her shoulders and picked her way over the uneven ground to the gate. There were a surprising number of locks on the gate, although all, except one, hung uselessly from the cold bars. Sarah fished for the huge bunch of keys Moore had handed her. She hoped she wouldn't have to sort through all of them. She looked at the padlock more closely. Scored into the metal was a strange symbol, a bit like a stylised twig with a circle around it. She ran her fingernail over it trying to remember why it seemed so familiar to her. As if of their own accord, her hand reached for the bunch of keys, and without hesitation pulled one out and fitted it into the lock with a satisfying *snick*.

Sarah rubbed her forehead in a gesture of bewildered worry, "I don't remember this," she muttered to herself. She pushed the gate open wide enough for her to slip through, and went on.

Her feet crunched on the gravel as she rounded a pair of sentinel pines. She knew the house was just up ahead, but she kept her gaze on the ground in front of her. She halted, took a deep breath, and raised her head.

The house was huge and grey, with lead lighted windows that stared back blankly. Ivy covered a good portion of the wall, its questing fingers tapping mournfully on some of the windows. There were turrets and gables and well, Sarah wasn't really sure about the architectural details, but she knew the house was grand. She barely registered the fact that she had fallen to her knees, and it wasn't until her vision swam that she realised she was crying. An ache deep inside her, so constant and dull she didn't even know it was there had flared to life as the tears tracked down her face. *I'm home.*

Eventually the gravel under her knees grew painful, and she pulled herself to her feet, still euphoric. She wiped her eyes and fumbled for the keys. She couldn't get into the building fast enough. She flicked on the lights out of a habit she didn't know she had. The dim bulbs did little to penetrate the gloom, but Sarah didn't notice. Her mind was awash with images, remembered or imagined, and she practically flew down the dusty corridors, opening doors and peering into rooms.

Spring; the doors were flung open, the scent of flowers and sunshine distracting as she tried to study. Summer; maids were hanging out billowing white sheets as the master's daughter danced laughing between them. Workmen carefully carrying an antique clock up the stairs. Glittering guests arriving for a party. A Christmas spent alone and wondering. A grave festooned with flowers, and a warm hand holding hers,

"You will be protected."

Eventually the tide of emotion subsided, and Sarah collapsed into a chair in what appeared to be a drawing room, unbothered by the cloud of dust that rose as she did so. This was certainly unexpected, this visceral attachment to a house she couldn't remember. Still, she felt safe here, and all the floors so far had been carpet or polished wood. No iron doors, no nightmares made real. Relief washed through her, although she could not say what she had been dreading. It was her father's house, and now it was her house. It just felt so right. She belonged. Safe. She curled up like a child, and fell asleep amongst the dust motes and memories.

It was nearly dark when she awoke. The trip in to the house seemed surreal, like a dream. What had she been thinking? Falling asleep in the middle of the day and sleeping here, of all places. *You're completely mad,* she told herself. She stretched and brushed the dust off her clothes. She supposed she should be getting back to the hotel, although she felt strangely reluctant to do so. It was if there was something she had missed, something she should see. She shook her head; this was meant to be a quick visit, not an expedition. She promised herself she'd come back.

She strode towards the front door, shutting doors and turning off lights. She started trotting towards the exit. The house might not have been the haunted mansion of her nightmares, but she didn't want to be here after dark.

With a sigh of relief she arrived back at the entrance hall. A spectacular staircase led up to the second floor, and Sarah looked around with pride.

With a house like this she felt like nobility, even if there wasn't a title to go with it.

The clouds had broken up while she was sleeping, and as she was about to leave a solitary beam of light filtered through the window and alighted on an oil painting, partly obscured by a curtain. Curious, she drew the curtain back.

It was a portrait. Sarah gasped, as her startled gaze met with her father's determined stare. She would not have recognised his face if it weren't for the subtle similarity to her own. His hair was the same pale gold, and the line of his nose matched hers. He was dressed for hunting, and he held a rifle in the crook of his arm. A gold cross hung at his throat. It was with a shock that Sarah realised he was standing in a graveyard. The background was vague, but she could make out urns and crosses silhouetted against an evening sky. There was no year or signature on the portrait that she could see, although there was a legend inscribed into the wooden frame.

Michael Berkley: Master of the Hunt

Sarah looked at the portrait again, and felt her fear return. This was her father? There was something decidedly creepy and otherworldly about the painting. It was as if the artist had rendered more than should be realised by mere paint. She shivered as she gazed into his eyes, for the unnamed artist had captured a strange light in them. Her father had seen things that were not meant to be seen. Her attention strayed to the legend again...*Hunt.* He had sought these things out, she knew.

She didn't know how long she stood in front of the painting, trying to get it to mesh with her fragmented memories. Eventually she pulled herself away from the image, and realised that there were two things she should have been paying more attention to. That the sun had set completely, and that she was no longer alone.

Chapter 2

"Your father was the best, you know. The world lost a great deal when he died." The words rolled down the stairs and spread themselves across the room like thunder. Sarah jumped with a frightened squeak and backed away from the painting, her eyes wide.

There was a man at the top of the stairs, his face in shadow. Sarah blinked into the dark. Eventually she found her voice, although it was much higher and more uncertain than she would have liked. "Who are you? What are you doing in my house?" She wished she'd brought one of her guns.

The stranger walked forward with an easy, predatory grace. He was tall and long-limbed, wearing a fitted, grey suit with a long coat that curled about his heels like smoke. He had long, dark hair that fell unbound past his broad shoulders.

Sarah didn't realize she was staring, but he appeared to. He stood at the top of the stairs, letting her gaze wander over him. He started walking down the stairs, looking pleased that he had her full attention. He ran long, pale fingers along the banister, his gaze never leaving her face.

It wasn't until he reached the bottom of the staircase that Sarah realized he hadn't answered her questions. She took a half-step back, and repeated her inquiry.

He smiled at her. It was a wide, lazy smile, insolent and provocative. Sarah could feel her heart hammering in her chest as she tried to stare him down. He stared back, still smiling, his eyes gleaming with mischief. She had thought they were brown at first, but now he was closer she realized that they were a deep red. She felt her nerve begin to crack; didn't he need to blink? She told herself that she was in her house, that she was a champion pistol shot and a grown woman, and she wasn't about to let herself be stared down by some squatter. None of it really helped. There was a dark aura of power about this man, a power she was helpless against. She tried to calculate how many steps away from the door she was.

His gaze dropped, to her infinite surprise. He swept gracefully into a low bow. "My name is Grimalkin, and I am bound to this house."

His voice was rich and deep, those simple words sending a shiver along her spine. She gaped stupidly, trying to think how to respond.

"This...this is *my* house."

"And thus I am bound to you..." that smile again, it made her heart skip a beat... "my Master."

He had waited so long, blind to the world outside the high walls surrounding the estate. He had feared--but his fears were groundless, for she was here. Real and alive and warm and so wonderfully--no. His teeth clicked together inside his mouth. He must not think like that, no matter how many years it had been.

He hadn't been able to see her, really see her, until that moment. Forced to content himself with vague reflections in dusty mirrors, he took the opportunity to observe her, examine her, and commit every mote of dust in her hair to memory as she had stood entranced by her father's image. She had a strong face, like her father. *What have you seen in the world?* he wondered. Her beauty was understated and enchanting; her hair flowing down her back, pale as the moon, her eyes a clear blue, so unlike his own. He thought about running his fingers through that hair, making those eyes flutter closed, tilting her head back to expose that lovely pale neck. His crimson eyes narrowed in frustration. Her charms would not be so captivating if she wasn't completely inaccessible.

She was speaking again, her tone less scared. *Don't fear me, Sarah,* he thought. *I cannot hurt you.*

"The lawyer didn't mention you. What exactly is your job?"

"Of course he didn't. There are secrets in every family, and yours has more than most." He bowed again. "And I am one of those secrets."

"You mean you've been living here all along?" she asked incredulously.

He chuckled. "I wouldn't say *living* exactly. But I have been forbidden to step outside of this estate, it is true." He could tell his cryptic answers were annoying her, and why not? It was a rather childish way of holding power over her, but a centuries-old vampire had his pride. She had lost her fear for now, it seemed. Her forehead wrinkled adorably as she paced up and down, trying to make sense of his answers.

"Why didn't Mrs. Cox know you were here?"

"Who? Oh, the toad-lady. I am always asleep when she arrives, and she only has access to rooms on the top levels."

"Toad-lady?"

"And that slimy husband of hers. You'd do well to fire them both; they've been doing a terrible job."

Sarah rubbed her temples. "I have no idea what is going on."

His smiled, a touch contemptuously. "You don't remember much, do you?" It disappointed him, what the Berkley family had been reduced to. She'd have to do better than that to be worthy of a servant such as him.

Sarah stared blankly out the window, her face in shadow. "I was in therapy for three years," she said quietly. He had the grace to look ashamed, but she didn't notice. He could see her letting her anger build, and even though he knew he was to be the target, he awaited the result with anticipation.

"I don't remember my parents. I don't remember this house. All I remember is pain and fear and darkness. I didn't let it beat me then, and by God I'm not going to let it beat me now. You," she turned and stabbed her index finger viciously into his chest, "are going to stop playing games. You are going to tell me everything. And if you're lucky, I won't haul your sorry squatter ass down to the courthouse for trespassing!" She finished with a yell, her gaze furious and electric, and her breasts heaving.

Grimalkin felt both chastised and elated. Now *this* was more like it.

Sarah glared up at him; his face was inches from her own. A small part of her brain was jumping up and down and asking her what the hell she was doing and why wasn't she running for the police. The rest of her mind was reveling in this feeling of strength. When she had first felt his presence she had been instinctively aware of his dark power. Now her perception shifted, and she felt the power within herself.

"Master," that word again fell from his sensual lips.

She shivered as she realized she liked the way it sounded. She wanted him to say it again. She found her gaze tracing the line of his jaw, sweeping across the lines of his lips that twitched with dark amusement, following the strands of dark hair- she realized it was a peculiar smoky grey- that gently brushed his cheek. He was mesmerizing. She had never seen a man so strange and alluring.

He seemed neither uncomfortable nor amused by her scrutiny. She had half expected that he would laugh at her, or at least bestow a wide gleeful grin upon her. He didn't. Instead he looked into her eyes with an intensity that made her ache inside. His lips parted fractionally, and she found herself copying him. Suddenly he exhaled with an infinitesimal shake of his head. He took a step back, and the connection was broken.

"Master," he said again, but this time it was distant, establishing a boundary between them. She was his master, and it was not his place to stand too close. She tucked a strand of hair back behind her ear, ignoring a flash of disappointment. She didn't really want to be this close to a complete stranger, she told herself. Her behavior had been asking for trouble, she knew. Sarah Berkley was a sensible woman who wouldn't even *think* of pressing her mouth to his, and running her hand through his hair while the other fumbled with that endless row of buttons, to pull back and watch those crimson eyes burn...

"Everything." His voice brought her out of her illicit daydream.

His attention was on her father's portrait, she was relieved to note. He probably hadn't seen her glassy expression.

"Everything is rather a lot to tell," he continued, "and while I have no problem with staying up all night..." He trailed off, further comment rendered superfluous by Sarah's stomach, which decided to remind her that she hadn't eaten anything since breakfast.

"One question." Sarah was not going to leave empty-handed.

Grimalkin inclined his head to show he was listening.

"What are you?" she asked.

"Now that's a question with many answers. Some of them are even true." He was grinning again.

"Give me the one that's most relevant. And if you try and be funny, I assure you things will go badly for you." A note of warning entered her voice.

"I'm a vampire," he said, his grin wider than ever. "Is that relevant enough for you?"

"You...you're kidding," she accused, although she couldn't work up much conviction.

He gave her a you-should-know-better look and flicked a speck of dust off his sleeve. "There are any number of entertaining ways to prove it to you. However, I shall abandon my dignity and use the simplest." So saying, he drew back his lips in something resembling a snarl. He opened his jaws and Sarah stifled a scream, for his incisors were a good inch longer than the rest of his teeth and wickedly pointed.

Pure instinct took over. Sarah bolted; it was only three desperate, pumping strides to the door. Her feet skidded on the dusty wood. He got there first, of course. He moved so fast she barely saw him.

A hundred and thirty pounds of adrenaline-fueled woman slammed into his chest. Grimalkin snarled in anger, not at her, but at himself. He couldn't resist a dramatic scene, and now he had frightened her out of her wits. She drew her arm back and punched him in the stomach. He didn't even flinch, but he felt that he deserved it. He held his hands up, and bowed his head in submission.

"I won't hurt you!" he snarled. She backed off, looking for another exit. "I'm sorry," he said in a softer tone. That got her attention. *Women love being apologized to*, he thought. In this case, she deserved it. She still looked like she was going to bolt. He stepped away from the door, his hands still raised. "I didn't mean to scare you...that much. I told you. I'm bound to this house. Sarah, I am your slave." He had finally said it. It cut him deeply, but it was the unvarnished truth. *So much for a vampire's pride,* he thought.

Sarah shook her head, trying to make sense of all that had happened. Her breath seemed to stick in her throat. "I need air," she managed to get out. She walked quickly, her gaze on the floor. She was at the doorway when his voice halted her once more.

"You will come back?" It was a question, not an order, and the naked desperation in his burning eyes pulled at her with frightening intensity. All she could do was nod once, and flee wordlessly into the night.

The stone-flagged floor was cold against her bare feet. She was no longer wounded, no longer afraid. She was no longer twelve, either. It was with a curious sort of detachment that she noticed she was naked. The cold air pinched her nipples hard and nipped at her ears. There was warmth up ahead, she knew, and she hurried forward eagerly.

The floor had changed to polished wood, and the full moon shone down through lead lighted windows. She hurried through the barred light, to a wooden door that stood ajar at the end of the corridor. She ran her fingers along the carved lines briefly, savoring the moment she arrived at her destination.

He was waiting for her, as she knew he would be. He standing with his back against the cold glass of the window; the moonlight spilling onto his hair made it glow blue. The room was warmer than the corridor, as the dream had promised, but the ache in her nipples did not subside. When he turned to face her, and the moonlight revealed that he too was unclothed, the ache went straight to her groin.

He stepped towards her, his fiery eyes burning into hers. She shivered in anticipation of his touch. He was so close! She could smell pine and night air and a hint of something dark and musky. Still she made no move towards him, as if her limbs had turned to lead. His pale hands moved across her shoulders, close enough to make her nerve endings scream, but never quite touching. He rested his fingertips lightly on her back, and gently urged her forward.

She fell towards him, her limbs free at last. He caught her in his cool, strong embrace. Her cheek rested against his chest, fine hairs tickling her heated skin. She ran her hands down his back, feeling the lines of muscle rolling beneath her fingers as his embrace tightened. His head bowed as he nuzzled her ear.

He nipped at her ear, gently but firmly pulling her towards the canopied bed that occupied the center of the room. She went more than willingly, pressing herself desperately against him. She felt him smile at her enthusiasm. Sarah panicked momentarily as she felt them fall, before realizing that they had made it to the bed. The impact of their landing made her breathless as she crashed into him.

He was done teasing. His hands roamed over her curves with abandon, and his breath was ragged in her ear. She writhed under his touch, desperate for more. She tangled her fingers through his hair, pulling herself up along his lean form. He bucked beneath her. Through a haze of desire she heard herself moan. He pulled her still higher and bent his head to her left breast. She gasped as she felt his fangs trail gently across the sensitive flesh. His lips closed, and he kissed the hard little nub, chastely, almost reverently. She whined wordlessly; she wanted more dammit!

With a snarl he relented, and effortlessly rolled them both. His hair fell across her cheek as he looked down at her. She could see in his face the effort of will it was taking to hold back, but he still managed to grin at her.

"Don't," she managed to pant out, "tease!" The moonlight illuminated enough of his face so she could see his mouth shape the word, "Master" although she heard no sound.

His eyes closed as he threw his head back. Yes! He was going to...

Sarah woke with a groan of frustration. She ached with lust and was covered in sweat. She flung herself back onto the pillow and one hand snaked down into her pajama pants. It was better than nightmares, she thought fuzzily, although just as disturbing in its own way. It wasn't until she eventually staggered out of bed to wash her face that the thought occurred to her. Even though she could see nothing but darkness she glared out the window towards Berkley Manor.

"You better not have done that deliberately, you bastard!"

The next day dawned cool and clear, and Sarah was planning an expedition. She packed food and clothes, as if she were going on a hike. Her pistol added a comforting weight to her bag. Maybe she was crazy, walking right back into the lair of a self-confessed predator. But it was *her* house. And, if Grimalkin was to be believed, he was hers as well.

She made the slow, bumpy drive up to the house. She didn't expect Grimalkin to be awake; she remembered that he had claimed to always be asleep when the housekeeper visited. Of course, she couldn't be sure. She had seen her fair share of horror movies, and had read a few vampire stories, but how many of the myths applied to beast that currently slumbered somewhere in her house?

Her father had carried a cross, but Grimalkin hadn't been bothered by it. She wondered if he could stand silver, or garlic, or wooden stakes. He slept during the day, but would sunlight kill him? Sarah got a strange sinking feeling when she realized that her shooting skills she was so proud of were probably useless. Then again, her father had carried a rifle.

Sarah didn't feel like going inside just yet, so she slung her pack over her shoulder and set off to explore the ruined garden. Crickets whirred out of her path as she waded through the tall grass. It wasn't until she was a fair way from the house that she wondered if there were any snakes.

No matter, she had her high hiking boots on today, and she was determined to explore her territory. The gardens had endured twelve years of neglect surprisingly well, for although exotic plants of all kinds had broken free of their beds, and weeds were growing untidily over everything, there were still traces of the original gardener's vision. It was glimpsed in the rows of trees and in the low stone benches -now overrun with vines- that offered the occupant a view carefully assembled for maximum impact.

Sarah passed under crumbling stone archways, and picked her way around fountains, now dry and full of leaves. It made her heart ache to see such beauty neglected. This was her world, and it had been abandoned. She found herself vowing to restore it to its former glory.

She rounded some topiary bushes, their original shapes long lost, and her breath caught. Enclosed by a wrought iron fence was a little cemetery. She stepped forward reverently. Like the gates to the central enclosure, the cemetery gate was encrusted with locks. Most of the locks were engraved with some kind of symbol.

Sarah had her keys, but she decided against unlocking the gate for now. She did not know if the locks were designed to prevent people getting in, or to prevent things getting out. Her world now encompassed real, if not live, vampires, and she wondered what other marvels lurked in her family's estate.

She rested her forehead against the iron bars, feeling more alone than she ever had before. The bright and noisy foster home she had spent her teenage years in seemed far away and distant, like a dream. She wondered who she really was. The estate had cast some kind of spell over her, making her feel at home, but she didn't feel quite herself anymore. She didn't feel like leaving either. Her previous existence, when viewed from this fantastical place, was about as enticing as a bowl of dead cockroaches.

She wondered why she had always felt so driven, but lacking in direction. She had poured her soul into her studies, and when they had ended she transferred her obsession to the pistol range. No time for parties, or romance. She felt herself blush as she remembered the dream. He implied he'd do anything she asked, but she couldn't ask him to do, well, *that*. She'd die of embarrassment first. The thought teased her; *maybe it would be worth it.*

She shook her head, and forced her mind onto less dangerous topics. Like just what had Grimalkin been eating all these years? Okay, so maybe not a less dangerous topic, but certainly a less palatable one. Presumably he hadn't been attacking Mrs. Cox. He seemed to regard her visits as an intrusion more than anything else. *Maybe blood drinking was just a myth*, she thought hopefully. No, she had to admit those fangs weren't just for decoration. *Although they did apparently have their uses*, she mused, her mind drifting back to the dream. Bloody hell, what was wrong with her today? *Try and keep the blood above waist level*, she reprimanded herself.

She had drifted away from the cemetery and walked up the grassy slope to the main house. She dumped her bag in the kitchen, which was presumably on Mrs. Cox's rounds, for it was relatively clean. Making the most of the sunlight, she started systematically exploring the top floors of the house.

She had expected the attic to be full of strange and wonderful things, and was slightly disappointed to discover it mainly held boxes of old clothes and dusty paperbacks. Sarah noted that there were no personal belongings up here, any dairies or photographs. If it weren't for the portrait in the entrance hall, there would have been no clue as to whose house it was.

She went through the rooms quickly, for there was little of interest. Everything was so impersonal she began to wonder if Mrs. Cox had been making off with any family trinkets. Most of the furniture was shrouded in dust sheets, but those she took the time to examine looked antique. Nothing yet that could be worth twelve million dollars, though.

In the excitement of meeting Grimalkin she had all but forgotten the money. She frowned, mentally cataloguing all she had seen. Just where were these 'antiquities and curios' that were worth so much money? It would make sense to have them locked up. She made a note to ask Grimalkin and continued on.

She wandered around what were presumably the family's quarters. There was a child's room, complete with a small bed and a writing desk, but she couldn't remember living there. *How strange*, she thought. It made her sad, the idea that the girl who had lived here had just died, with no connection to the woman who now stood in her place.

Her head full of melancholic thoughts, Sarah did not pay much attention to the next room she visited until she found herself looking out the window. The very same window that had spilled moonlight over Grimalkin in her dream. She stepped back and glanced around the room in alarm. While the bed was covered in a white dust sheet, this room was definitely the same as the one in her dream. The master bedroom. She felt a surge of anger towards the vampire; he *must* have been causing that dream after all. Her hands clenched in anger. She just wanted to...just wanted to... *Dammit. Get out of my mind!* she thought, livid that her headspace had been invaded.

Still fuming, she strode down the stairs, determined to find Grimalkin's lair and give him the most unpleasant awakening of his unlife. Or stab him through the heart with a wooden umbrella handle.

She found a flight of stairs leading below ground, and with her keys jangling in one hand and a flashlight in the other in case the power went out she stormed down. It wasn't until she'd passed a wall sconce with cracked decoration three times that she realized she was going in circles. The underground complex was at least as large as the house that sat above it.

Every door was locked, although most had brass plaques screwed into them with interesting names like *Mayan Chest One* and *Siberia Train 1947*.

Sarah felt uneasiness creep over her, but she was determined to find the vampire she was now sure lived down here. It was still daylight up there somewhere, so he had to be asleep. She went back to the foot of the stairs and tried again, this time making careful note of the turns she made.

Sarah found herself in a new corridor, every door of iron. She felt the fear clawing at her throat, but she pushed it down.

"Be strong, Sarah," she mumbled shakily to herself. "This is your house."

The doors still had plaques attached, but the legend on each of them was the same--*Sealed,* followed by a year. Some of the doors had been welded shut, and some had apparently been papered over.

Dim bulbs dangled from the ceiling, but Sarah switched on her torch anyway. She knew there was paved stone under her feet, but she refused to look at it, instead fixing her eyes on the endless row of *Sealed* doors.

Her foot struck something metallic. Instinctively she looked down, and for a few seconds she blinked at the object near her foot. The pistol was rusted and dusty, and obviously hadn't been touched for years. She frowned at it. In the back of her head lurked an explanation for its presence.

Her eyes focused on the floor and the strange brownish substance that had been spilled on it...*blood*...her mind supplied the detail. Her head pounded in time with her fluttering heart. She felt sick. She turned to run, all thoughts of her previous mission forgotten. She had made it but two steps when her vision darkened, and the stained stone appeared to rush up toward her.

Chapter 3

He watched Sarah shiver as a cold breeze brushed her face and she snuggled closer. Grimalkin smiled a genuine smile of relief; she was all right. She would awaken soon, and he would have to let her go. His arms tightened instinctively around her at the thought.

He had sensed her indistinctly through the feet of iron and concrete that had separated them. The sun had still been hanging low over the horizon, and he had continued dreaming. Until her consciousness had winked out, like the last star before dawn. That had wakened him, although he was slow and uncoordinated.

He had crawled out of what he optimistically termed a coffin and had stumbled and reeled out into the corridor. It was practically suicide, taking on any opponent with sunlight still feet above his head, but his first priority was to protect his master. Sun-blunted senses straining to detect any enemy, he had lurched along the corridor, supporting himself on the wall.

There hadn't been any opponent, just his flaxen-haired master, lying on the floor in a dead faint. He had collapsed beside her, cautious relief coursing through him. He knew she was alive, he could sense her pulse feet away, and she wasn't bleeding. Carefully and gently he had run his fingers over her head, looking for more subtle injuries. Finding none, he had let her head rest on his arm and waited silently for the sun to set.

His eye had fallen on the pistol. Was she scared of guns? It seemed like an overreaction even so. He had known it was there, but had never paid it much attention. Like the rest of the objects in the house, he wasn't allowed to touch it. He wasn't allowed to touch *her* either. Grimalkin wasn't one to follow the rules if he could get away with it.

He wasn't breaking the rules, technically. She was in some kind of danger, and that consideration overruled all others. Checking for injuries was well within the bounds of his pact. A case could be made for carrying her up to the fresh air. Cradling her in his arms until she woke up was probably stretching it. He knew he was making it worse, but he couldn't help himself. She was so beautiful and so *alive*. She was so pale she might have passed for one of his kind, but she was warm, she walked in the sunlight. He had dreamt of her, and in his dreams she had been warm.

You've been sucking on rats too long, he told himself. *The first warm-blooded girl walks past and you're acting like you were turned last week.* It was undignified, he decided, and he did his best to muster up his usual contempt for the living. He *was* higher in the food-chain, and it was only though the agency of powerful magic that she was his master. It was totally unnatural, he decided, the irony not lost on him.

Her father hadn't quite pulled out all the stops to kill him. He still didn't know why. Michael *could* have killed him; he had the knowledge and the power. Instead he had sealed the vampire beneath his house, bound him in dozens of different ways, and left him to rot. Grimalkin knew that if events had fallen differently he would still be down there in the sterile dark. Still going mad. He owed her everything. And everything was what she was going to get.

He studied her face, her fingers tangled in the folds of his coat, her hair falling across his arm. She shivered in her sleep again and pulled herself closer. Her warmth was delicious against his chest and her weight across his lap--he shifted uncomfortably; this was definitely not the time to get horny.

He looked out across the darkened estate. The news was traveling, even now, that a Berkley had returned. It mattered little that the Berkley knew next to nothing about her family's duty, or about the world her family had inhabited. He shook his head; this wasn't going to be easy for either of them. He wondered why he should care, for if she died he would be free. The answer was immediate; he did care, and that was that. Why or how exactly he cared he didn't know, and it probably didn't matter.

He felt himself being watched; his gaze flicked down to meet that of the woman in his arms. He smiled. "It's all right. You're safe." He half expected her to shriek at him or slap him, but instead she slowly disentangled herself from his embrace and stood up. "Are you feeling all right?"

"I'm just a little confused. I was scared. I was looking for you- You!" She seemed to have recovered remarkably quickly, her tone infused with anger. "Can you mess with people's heads?" She stepped backwards.

"Hey! Whoa!" His long arm shot out and he caught her wrist. "It's quite a way to fall."

She looked about her. "Grimalkin, why are we on the roof?"

"You needed fresh air." He shrugged. "Besides, I like roofs." He watched her scramble away from the edge and sink down onto the tiles, two feet of space separating them.

"Answer my earlier question, slave." She was still irritated, obviously. "Can you mess with my mind?"

"I'm sorry. I just nudged you to sleep. There was no other way to get you to stay until dark. Frankly I didn't think you'd notice."

Sarah stared at him. Grimalkin raised an eyebrow. Wasn't that what she meant?

She licked her lips nervously "So, it wasn't you who made me feel...uhh..."

He suddenly noticed she was blushing.

"...those feelings of coming home?" she finished quickly.

"You overestimate my talents. You did *that* on your own." He supposed some reassurances were in order. "I can't read your mind, Master." She always looked at him strangely when he said that word. "There are vampires out there who also study magic, and I suppose they could. That's probably where the myth comes from."

"Ok, then, let's approach this logically. What exactly *can* you do?"

"I am stronger, faster, and have keener senses than any human. At night. During the day I'm a lot less fierce. I've never studied magic." He smiled. "I never had the patience. So I can't cast any spells, nor do any fancy tricks like that. I have...a kind of power, but it's uncontrolled. The magic that binds me to you also binds them. You can release them temporarily, although I should warn you that while you are safe, no one else will be."

Sarah listened intently; she took a deep breath and asked, "What can hurt you?"

"Sanctified objects are more efficacious. Silver stings like you wouldn't believe. Sunlight...I'm all but helpless during the day. Sunlight burns, but I do not know how long it would take to kill me. There are various forms of magic that will harm me. Warm blood will revive me, the greater the damage, the more I need."

"Blood..." She shivered. "What have you been living on all these years?"

"Animals. And the occasional trespasser."

"Did you kill them?"

"Of course I did. A wound to the jugular vein isn't that easy to treat and assuming they did survive there would be a chance they'd be infected. One vampire in the area is enough. Besides, human blood to me is like the finest nectar. I wasn't about to waste any."

Sarah looked vaguely ill. *She'll have to get used to it*, he thought. There were far worse things out there than him. Besides, he wanted her to accept him. It was highly unlikely that she could look upon his true nature unflinchingly, but he could dream. That part of him that was still human was achingly lonely.

She watched the moonrise. He watched her. She had assimilated a lot in quite a short space of time. Perhaps she would adapt better than he'd thought. She closed her eyes and breathed deep of the night air.

"I feel so alive," she said wonderingly.

He smiled; she obviously hadn't sat under the stars for a long time.

"Cherish that feeling," he said quietly.

She looked over at him, her eyes wide. "I'm sorry, I didn't mean to offend."

"You didn't." There was a peaceful silence between them as they watched the moon for a little longer. Grimalkin felt strangely warmed by the knowledge; for now she trusted him. For now she was happy to sit in the moonlight with him. For now, that was enough.

Eventually she turned back to him, regretfully breaking the silence. "I'm hungry. I brought some food, but it's down in the kitchen. How do we get down?"

"We jump. Or rather, I jump. I can carry you or you can ride on my back."

She frowned, glancing around in case there was another way down. Grimalkin did his best to convince himself that he didn't carry her up there so he'd have to carry her down. Eventually he said, "I could get you a ladder. There's probably one around somewhere."

She glanced over the edge of the roof and hurriedly backed away from it. Grimalkin twitched; was he really that repulsive?

"Carry me," she said finally, looking rather shamefaced.

He felt slightly guilty for putting her through this, and he vowed not to indulge himself at her expense again. At least, he vowed to try.

He stepped up to her, somewhat awkwardly. She was carefully not meeting his eyes. Her heart rate had picked up. Interesting, he thought, although she was probably scared about jumping off a three-story building. He hesitated for a second, and then in one smooth movement effortlessly picked her up, bridal style. She squeaked and rather cautiously put her arm around his neck. She still wasn't meeting his eyes.

He stepped to the edge. She glanced over again then hastily shut her eyes. Her other arm snaked around his neck and she buried her face in his shoulder.

"It will be all right," he reassured her.

"Just get it over," she said, her voice muffled against his coat. He obeyed. He leapt gracefully off the edge, his long hair streaming out behind him. She tensed in his arms, braced for impact. There was a solid thump as he hit the ground. His tall frame absorbed the impact easily, and he straightened, his master still in his arms.

Sarah pulled away from his coat, her arms still around his neck. She glanced around cautiously, then back at him.

"We made it."

He smirked. "Don't sound so surprised. Of course we did." He could feel her warm breath against his chin as her gaze raked his face.

She gave a tremulous little laugh. "I'm sorry I missed it."

"We could do it again, if you like," he suggested, his voice laced with dry humor.

"No!" she said hastily. "No. That will be fine." Her heartbeat quickened as she looked into his eyes. Grimalkin felt a knowledgeable smile curve his lips. So she *was* reacting to his proximity. He knew he was reacting to hers. Perhaps, she wasn't so inaccessible after all. Suddenly she seemed to come to her senses, and she removed her arms from his neck. Without comment he gently lowered her feet to the ground. She touched his shoulder briefly.

"Thank you," she said, a blush staining her cheeks and then she was trotting back towards the house. With a shake of his head, the vampire followed her inside.

Sarah busied herself searching through her bag for the food she had packed. Her heartbeat was returning to normal, but she still tingled where he had held her. His grip had been so gentle and strong. She felt a smile curve her lips, unbidden, at the thought. She tried to summon up her previous fear, but couldn't. With the vampire, *her* vampire, she was safe. From outside forces, at least. As for the vampire himself, she didn't know what to think.

He prowled restlessly around the kitchen, peering out of windows like some caged beast. His constant movement was beginning to get on her nerves.

"Ham and salad sandwich?" she offered. He shook his head. "Oh, sorry. You can't eat normal food?"

"No more than you can eat rocks," he replied, poking at a spider web critically. "I told you Mrs. Cox was doing a bad job."

"You're not going to...eat anything?" she asked, rather nervously.

"Not unless you order me to."

"Oh, I wouldn't do *that*."

He turned and gazed at her fixedly. "Why not?" His tone was practically accusatory.

"Because...because it's not my place to."

He rounded the kitchen table and dropped into the chair next to hers. "Let me explain something to you, Master. I am not your employee. I am not your butler. I'm not your guardian angel, either. I am your slave. If you desire me to eat, I will eat. If you desire me to kill, I will kill. If you desire me to do *this--*" Sarah jumped as Grimalkin, in a move so fast she could barely follow it, tore a knife from the rack attached to the cupboard and slammed it though his hand that rested on the table and into the dark timber beneath. "I will do it."

Sarah stared in horror at the blade. Her frightened gaze flicked up to Grimalkin's face. His jaw was set, his lips pulled into a thin line. His posture was challenging, but not threatening. His gaze was intense as he gauged her reaction.

Sarah took a rather shaky breath and wrapped her hands around the handle of the knife. With some difficulty she pulled it free from the woodwork and from Grimalkin's hand. There was a faint red smear on the blade, but the wound healed almost instantaneously. Sarah laid the knife aside thoughtfully.

"How do you feel about this?"

He swallowed. "What?"

Her gaze locked with his. "How do you feel about being my slave, Grimalkin?"

He seemed genuinely taken aback.

Sarah mentally awarded herself a point.

"It hurts my pride," he admitted finally. "I am so old I don't remember my original name or nationality. You are just a slip of a human girl..."

"I understand your feelings. However," her eyes flashed in the dim light, "I don't particularly like the way you keep trying to scare, or test me or whatever it is you think you're doing. I *know* you can't hurt me." She gave a proud and imperious smile. "So I'm not scared of you, Mr. High-And-Mighty-Vampire. And if you're not careful," she leaned forward smugly, "I might forget my good nature and order you to do something really nasty."

His eyes gleamed, and he smiled widely, his anger apparently forgotten. He leaned forward until his mouth was next to hers. Sarah felt her cheeks heat up.

"Something really nasty? You never know, I might just enjoy it."

Sarah pulled herself back so fast her chair nearly overbalanced. "I didn't mean...that kind of nasty," she said in a rather strangled tone.

Grimalkin grinned as he watched her blush, then stretched and wandered away, letting her eat her frugal dinner in peace. Sarah could sympathize with his plight to a certain extent, but his mood swings were extremely annoying. Not to mention his innuendo and almost constant invasion of her personal space. Not that Sarah would have minded if the sexy vampire had appeared to be serious about it. In her experience boyfriends weren't worth the trouble, but a *slave*. Well, who wouldn't be tempted?

But she couldn't read him. There was a nagging fear in the back of her mind that he was laughing at her. He might not be able to physically harm her, but if she allowed him to get too close--he could break her heart, she knew. Inadvertently, the very fact that she existed was a blow to his pride. And what she had seen of him so far did not bode well for his moral or mental stability.

"I thought vampires were supposed to be cool and collected. Not subject to violent mood swings," she called out irritably.

Grimalkin seemed to materialize out of the shadows in the corner of the kitchen, his smirk still firmly in place. "And I thought human women were supposed to be dressed in flimsy nightgowns and have heaving bosoms. At least, that's what I learned from the *movies*," he said rather contemptuously.

"You see movies?"

"Well, I did when I was free. I don't get out much nowadays."

Sarah rolled her eyes at his sarcasm and cleared away the remains of her dinner. "Well I'm sorry I disappoint you, not being the type to wear flimsy nightgowns and all."

"I never said it was a disappointment." He was smiling again.

Foiled. What *was* he thinking?

"Joking aside," he sounded more serious now, "there are some things that you really need to know about your family."

"There's nothing here, that's for sure." Sarah rubbed her hand absentmindedly against her chin.

"I'm not quite sure what you mean."

"In this entire house there is nothing. No pictures, no diaries, no nothing. It's empty. It's just got...stuff. Stuff that could belong to anyone."

"Well spotted. I gather you can't remember anything of your childhood?"

"Just standing in front of a grave. I think it was my mother's."

"I see. I shall do my best to explain what I know. Please remember, however, that your father and I were adversaries, not confidants. I can only give you an outsider's view."

"Thank you." Sarah bit her lip, and waited.

"From what I gather, the Berkley's are an old family. You will probably find out more about their history from family papers--wait please. There *are* family papers and such, but they are in one of the vaults below the house. There's probably some mind-numbingly sad and noble story as to how your family fell into its eternal duty, but I don't know it. All I know is that you come from a long line of powerful and distinguished alchemists, mystics, magicians and adventurers. What they were grooming you for I don't know. Your father was a powerful fighter. He had to be. He bested me, after all."

"Naturally," Sarah said dryly, although she was fascinated.

"They collected...things; objects and entities that could be dangerous, and stored them safely away from the world. Within certain circles they were famous. Even I'd heard of them, although I couldn't have cared less. There are many people who would love to get their hands on the Berkley collection, so they took extreme measures to prevent anyone gaining power over them. Hence all personal correspondence is kept in the vaults."

"So *that's* where the twelve million dollars is."

"To the right people, the collection could be worth a hundred times more than that. Hence the large number of charms and locks on the front gate."

"And the cemetery."

"You saw that did you? Yes, death can be less permanent than most would believe. I'm unliving proof of it. Your ancestors took steps to ensure their rest would be eternal. All part of the Berkley paranoia. Something *you* have to learn."

"Me? You can't expect me to do...whatever it is Berkley's are supposed to do."

"I don't have a say in it. I'm just a slave. It's the monsters baying outside the walls of the estate you must answer to."

"But...I'm a graphic designer, not Indiana Jones!"

"You need to give yourself more credit. And remember, you wield the most powerful weapon in the country."

"I do? What?"

"Me, of course," Grimalkin grinned arrogantly.

"Modest, aren't you?" Sarah sighed. "I guess...I guess I couldn't expect all this to come for free."

"The job has some perks."

"You again, I suppose," Sarah said skeptically.

"That's very nice of you to say so." Grimalkin smoothed out an imaginary wrinkle in his coat. "But I was actually referring to the job itself. If you don't die, I gather it's quite enjoyable. Plenty of opportunity to travel."

"I've..." Sarah smiled uncertainly, "I've always liked airports."

"You can afford a private jet now," he prompted.

"I'm not *that* wealthy."

"Oh, really? I think you'll find there's quite a bit to this inheritance that the lawyer didn't know about."

"You're telling me."

Grimalkin let her sit and absorb the information. Sarah didn't feel that she was absorbing it very well. It was like a dream, or a movie. She'd wake up and life would be ordinary again. She picked at the cut Grimalkin had made earlier in the wooden table, her mind swirling. She wondered what Rebecca would say, and then immediately felt a stab of guilt for ignoring her friend for the best part of...was it only a week? It seemed like a lifetime.

"Why did you fight my father?" Sarah asked, finally voicing the question that had been nibbling at her consciousness.

"I knew we'd get to this," Grimalkin muttered to himself. He gave a tight, humorless smile. "I made too much noise."

"What?"

"I caused trouble. I like to play with my food. I don't get along with other vampires. Eventually some of the old undead families tried to have me killed. It didn't work. They went to your father, making a case that I was too dangerous to walk free, even by vampire standards. The rest, as they say, is history."

"What did you *do*?"

"To the other vampires? You have to understand, Master, that vampires get very bored. So they make up games and have feuds, and generally act like the inbred snobs that they are."

"Inbred?"

"Well not technically," he waved his hand, "but their bloodlines are so important to them. I have no bloodline at all. I can't remember being turned, let alone who turned me. So of course I wasn't allowed to play."

"And my father agreed to hunt you? Why?"

"Your guess is as good as mine. Maybe the other vampires were right. Maybe he wanted a challenge. But that's not the point. You're the master of Berkley Manor now."

Sarah had the feeling that Grimalkin wasn't saying all that he knew, but decided not to press the issue. Not yet, not while they were getting along marginally well. She decided to wait until their next fight.

"I feel that none of this is very real to you." Grimalkin's deep, silky voice broke into her thoughts. "I don't wish to rush, but if you're game..." He trailed off, a seductive smile on his face.

"Game for what?" Sarah said warily.

"Hunting." His eyes practically glowed.

"What? People?" Sarah was horrified.

"We'll work up to them. I was thinking more of the creatures that patrol the edge of your estate so diligently."

"What creatures? Why are they here?"

"They're mostly mindless. Occasionally your father would clear them away. They're drawn by the power they can sense residing here. No threat. Not while we're in here."

"Are they dangerous?"

"Yes. But do not fear, Master." Grimalkin stood and held out his hand. "I will protect you with all of my strength and power."

Who could resist? Mesmerized, Sarah placed her small hand into his large one, as if accepting the offer of a dance. Grimalkin bowed graciously and led her deferentially out of the room, his red eyes gleaming in triumph.

Grimalkin hadn't fed for nearly two days now. This was a deliberate decision on his part. The thirst gnawed at him, making him strong and dangerous. His powers were fueled by the desire to hunt and kill. It had been such a long time since he had been free to fight; he wanted to show Sarah just how powerful he was.

His need for her was acute as well. The desire for blood and the desire for sex were closely linked for vampires. He told himself it was a side-effect that he could deal with, that he didn't *have* to watch her long legs as she strode in front of him or breathe longingly of her faint scent. She was so adorable when she blushed; and it was so easy to make her blush. He just wanted to crush her to him and bite- no, kiss, that was it. Of course she would have a fit if he could and did do anything of the sort.

Grimalkin had never been a patient person. Though he technically had eternity he always wanted things *now*. Now he was being forced to wait, possibly fruitlessly, for his master to see his full potential.

Somewhere inside the insecure graphic designer lurked a Berkley. The fact that she was no longer afraid of him proved the point, as far as he was concerned. Whether she knew it or not, she was more afraid of her own responses to him. He smiled to himself; he was going to have to get her over that fear soon. And now he had the opportunity to show off, have some fun, and just maybe get her to loosen up a little. His mouth watered at the thought.

Chapter 4

Sarah's boots tapped briskly on the wooden floor as she strode imperiously towards the front of the house, Grimalkin sauntering noiselessly behind her. She walked fast to hide her nervousness, and she jumped when Grimalkin laid a hand on her arm to steer her down one of the flights of stairs that led below the house.

"Wha- where are we going?" She couldn't keep the note of alarm from her voice.

Grimalkin chuckled in the dark, his laugh as dark and rich as treacle. "I wouldn't dream of letting you face any kind of danger unable to protect yourself."

"I can protect myself," Sarah said coolly, and pulled her pistol from her bag.

"You can use that?"

Sarah was gratified to hear the note of surprise in his voice. "Of course I can." She nearly rattled off a list of her marksmanship awards, but decided instead to let the vampire see for himself. He was obviously pushing her into this excursion so he could show off; well, two could play at that game.

"I would still suggest," he broke into her thoughts, "that you pick up something a little less...mundane."

"What do you mean?" Sarah asked as they arrived outside a steel reinforced door. Again unbidden, her fingers found the correct keys to open the set of three modern-looking locks.

"Well, this house doubles as a fortress..." Grimalkin pushed the heavy door open for her, "and every fortress has an armory."

Sarah's questing fingers found a light switch. Banks of fluorescents flickered on and she gasped. Neatly arranged and locked in banks of weapon racks were rows and rows of pistols, rifles, and blades of all kinds. Some were obviously antique but all were carefully stored and looked fully operational. In the corner of the room was a workbench with gunsmithing tools and down the far end of the armory was an armored car and a-

"It's a *tank*!" Sarah stared in amazement.

"That is to be used as a last resort. If the wards on some of the items break, or if all defenses fail, the tank has been warded to become a getaway vehicle, or so I understand."

Sarah wandered among the rows of weapons, half of which she couldn't even guess as to what their names were. She noticed a shoulder mounted rocket launcher and a stock of missiles in their own special case. She raised an eyebrow.

"Most of this stuff isn't legal you know."

"Neither is keeping slaves." Grimalkin shrugged. "The Berkleys have always played by their own rules."

"Wow." Sarah sat on the chair at the workbench. "This stuff is just so...cool. It's like the batcave or something."

"I'm glad you like it. I was going to suggest you take a shotgun, but since you claim to be competent with a pistol, how about one of these?" He pointed to a rack of handguns, ammunition stored neatly under each weapon.

"What's wrong with the pistol I already have?" Sarah walked over and unlocked the case.

"It hasn't, I assume, been modified to take down supernatural creatures."

"Silver bullets? Don't be ridiculous, silver would wreck your gun."

"Look, I don't use guns. I have no idea what your father shot me with. All I know is that it hurt like hell."

Sarah examined the weapons. Most of them had fine engraving on them; strange runes or little pictures. Sarah picked up a box of commercially made hollow-point ammunition. The bullets inside appeared to be standard, but someone had carefully placed something inside the hollowed out ends. It smelt faintly of mint.

"That would be your father's voodoo stuff." Grimalkin was waiting impatiently by the car.

"Voodoo?"

"Look, there's probably a recipe book in the bench somewhere. Can we get moving? You can examine this tomorrow if you must."

Sarah picked up a Walther P99, a favorite of law enforcement agencies, and a couple of boxes of ammunition. As an afterthought she also grabbed a pump action shotgun and familiarized herself with its operation as best she could without actually firing it.

Grimalkin managed to look bored and impatient, but she ignored him. It was like all her Christmases had come at once. It was her house and her inheritance, so she could take the time to enjoy it if she pleased.

To her surprise, Grimalkin tossed her the keys to the car and climbed into the passenger side. Sarah shot him a quizzical look and dumped her bag in the back seat.

"You drive, I fight." Grimalkin grinned widely at her, displaying his fangs.

Sarah shrugged and hit the button on the key ring labeled 'doors'. There was a humming sound and the wall slid back to reveal a short tunnel leading up to the surface.

"Huh. It still works." Grimalkin yawned, looking nonchalant and relaxed now that they were finally on their way.

Sarah shook her head as she put the car in gear; she'd never understand him, she thought.

The set of doors at the other end of the tunnel didn't open as easily. There was a horrible grating sound and they jammed halfway. Grimalkin wordlessly slid out of the car and with unnatural strength pushed them open wide enough for the vehicle to exit.

The tunnel ended somewhere in the forests of the estate. Sarah tried unsuccessfully to catch a glimpse of the house so she could get her bearings. There was a rough and overgrown track leading further into the woods. It hadn't been used in many years, and as Sarah eased the car forward, hanging branches brushed the roof and sticks and leaves crunched underneath the heavy-duty tyres.

Sarah managed to concentrate on her driving--she'd never driven anything so big and powerful before--although she was aware of Grimalkin looking at her from the corner of his eye. Since she had agreed to go on the mission he hadn't made any jokes, instead contenting himself with observing her. She guessed that she was still on trial. She'd show him. She'd kick ass, and he'd *have* to acknowledge her as...as...she didn't know what. A worthy master, perhaps, or a friend. Friend? *Him*? *When hell freezes*, she thought.

He irritated her beyond description, and yet she found herself enjoying his company. His presence was both challenging and reassuring, like no one else she had even known. He seemed to genuinely believe she could continue her family's work, although that seemed to be partly an extension of his own arrogance.

"Nervous?" he asked. Sarah glanced over quickly; to her surprise there was not a trace of sarcasm in his voice or eyes. Touched by his uncharacteristic gentleness, she smiled and shook her head. He smiled back, and suddenly the cabin of the car seemed very small and very close.

His long arm rested on the back of the seat, and Sarah's gaze fell approvingly on the way his coat stretched across his chest. Unconsciously she bit her bottom lip as she followed the creases in his neat grey trousers. It was definitely getting too hot in there, and Sarah had half a mind to turn the car around and exercise her authority, and maybe some other things.

His smoldering eyes regarded her face, a faint smile on his lips. He seemed to be enjoying her scrutiny, but was restricting his study of her to her face. Desire and nervousness coiled within her, a heady mixture that she hadn't experienced for quite a while. She licked her lips; her mouth was dry.

"Grimalkin?"

He was about to answer when something crashed into Sarah's side of the car with enough force to make its suspension rock. Sarah shrieked in fright, and her companion made a noise somewhere between a purr and a snarl. Sarah fumbled for the Walther and scrambled across the seat towards Grimalkin. Just outside the radius of the headlights were three pairs of pale, glowing eyes. Whatever it was that had charged the door, it had backed off again.

"They're here."

Sarah was shocked by the undisguised glee in Grimalkin's tone.

His fangs were bared and his eyes gleamed greedily. "I've waited years to have some fun." His words distorted around his oversized canines.

Sarah pulled away from him cautiously. She wasn't afraid of him, but she could imagine him hurting her accidentally in his eagerness to fight.

He tore his gaze away from the creatures outside. With an obvious effort of will he spoke calmly. "The roof."

Sarah glanced up. Behind the driver's seat was what appeared to be a sunroof. Despite his size, Grimalkin pulled himself over the front seat in one fluid motion. He shot the bolts that held the roof in place and opened the hatch. Sarah clambered over awkwardly, her nose practically brushing his coat.

He pulled himself up and out onto the roof. A second later he extended his hand to where Sarah crouched uncomfortably in the back of the car.

"Come out and watch," he urged.

Sarah gritted her teeth and grabbed the shotgun. Poking her head out cautiously, the first thing she saw was Grimalkin's big leather boot. She glanced up at the vampire, who was standing on top of the car, one foot perched on what appeared to be a mount for a machine gun. She could hear grunting and snarling in the darkness. She rubbed her hands nervously on her coat, and rechecked that the Walther was loaded.

At Grimalkin's insistence she clambered up to sit on the roof, although she was ready to bolt back into the safety of the car at any moment. Grimalkin knelt down beside her, and mouthed in her ear, "Don't be afraid."

Sarah had no time to reply, merely to notice Grimalkin reach down into the car and yank out a wire. Then the headlights died.

In the total blackness Sarah was too scared to even yell. Her free hand reached out and gripped Grimalkin's shoulder. She could feel him move as he looked around, and at one stage his long hair brushed lightly against her cheek.

"Can you see in the dark?" she whispered.

"Yes. Close your eyes, your night vision will return."

Sarah obeyed, her fingers still firmly gripping the vampire's shoulder. "All right."

"It's showtime."

Sarah opened her eyes. It was still too dark to make out much; then the moon came out.

The pale radiance flooded the scene, revealing the fact that somehow, without even noticing, Sarah had managed to drive through a stone wall. Sarah had no time to ponder the phenomenon; yet again something smashed into the side of the car.

Grimalkin dived off the roof and landed on something with a sickening crack. There was an animalistic groan and Sarah heard another impact, then silence. Gripping the Walther so tightly her knuckles were white, Sarah peered over the edge of the car.

Grimalkin was leaning nonchalantly against the armored plating. At his feet was a roughly humanoid form, two massive holes in its back. Grimalkin's hands were drenched in blood.

"Do you want to see it?" the vampire asked.

Sarah summoned her courage and nodded. Grimalkin reached down and grabbed the creature around its neck. As he pulled it up for her inspection, Sarah noticed its head was grossly oversized. It had huge, pale eyes and its mouth was big enough to swallow a watermelon whole.

"What is it?"

"It's a manifestation of greed or hunger that got in contact with something magical and grew a physical form. It has no mind, no purpose, other than to seek out magical power and consume it."

Grimalkin gave his little lecture seemingly unaware of the pale eyes that glowed in the dark behind him. He shook the corpse as if it were a puppet, a strange smile on his face. Were the eyes closer than before?

Sarah opened her mouth to warn him, shut it again and raised her gun. One set of eyes vanished. Sarah didn't hesitate; she smoothly squeezed the trigger twice, aiming at the darkness above Grimalkin's left shoulder. The vampire didn't as much as blink.

The eyes appeared again, but tilted to the side. There was a shuffling sound, and Grimalkin stepped to the side as another corpse landed at his feet.

"I got one!" Sarah yelled excitedly.

"Wasn't so difficult, was it?" Grimalkin grinned at her, dropping the first body with distaste.

"You knew it was there, didn't you?"

"Of course I did. I'm aware of the other one coming up behind me, too. I just wanted to see what you were made of."

The third creature attacked. Grimalkin was thrown against the side of the car by the creature's impact. Sarah raised her gun, but didn't want to risk hitting the vampire. Grimalkin pushed himself upright, the creature's needle-like teeth buried in his shoulder. With an arrogant smile he reached behind him and pulled the creature off. Sarah winced as his shoulder tore; the creature's teeth were buried deep. The wound closed almost immediately, and to Sarah's surprise his coat seemed to mend also.

The creature flailed about with its claws and tried to twist its head around to bite again. Grimalkin paid it no mind, his eyes locked with Sarah's. Sarah assumed he was going to wring the creature's spindly neck, but instead he *pulled*. The creature's eyes bugged and its long black tongue lolled.

Suddenly there was a nauseating pop, and the creature's head came free. Sarah shrieked and recoiled. Grimalkin raised an eyebrow and dropped the lifeless pieces.

"Don't be cruel!" Sarah yelled.

"They're not human. They're not even animals. They don't even have minds."

"I don't care. Kill them quickly, and that's an order, slave."

Grimalkin looked disappointed, but only for a moment. His wide smile soon returned, and Sarah wondered what he was up to.

"Quickly, you say. Why of course, Master. I just wonder how you are going to keep up."

"What do you mean?"

"Well, I suppose you could wait here for me."

"What? Where are you going?"

"To kill them quickly. I can't hang around waiting for them to shuffle over here. Well, I'm off."

"Wait. That wasn't what I meant!"

"It's what you said," he grinned.

"Don't you dare twist my words."

"But, Master, that's taking all the fun out of it."

"We're not here to have fun."

"Speak for yourself."

Sarah glowered at him. She took a deep breath and tried to calm down. There was no point in fighting him, she realized. It was time to polish her vampire management skills.

"What," she asked sweetly, "do you suggest we do?"

That seemed to cheer him up immediately, "Well, I have to protect you, of course, so I can't really leave you here. But the armored car is a bit big and unwieldy." He looked up at her with a strange expression. "Sarah, do you trust me?"

Sarah felt her breath catch. She had never heard him say her name before; she liked the way it fell from his lips. He was holding out his hand, his expression carefully blank. With trepidation she put her small, warm hand into his large, cool one.

"Yes," she said finally.

He smiled most of the time. Mocking, sarcastic, arrogant, amused--she had never seen him smile the way he smiled then. It was an affectionate smile, a smile that reached his eyes as his fingers closed gently around hers. It was a smile that touched something inside her and set it alight; small and oh, so warm. Without hesitation she reached out her arms and let him lift her off the car, effortlessly, as if she weighed nothing at all.

His hands remained on her upper arms for a while after her feet had touched the ground. What if he kissed her? The thought arrived unbidden in her head. Maybe he was thinking the same thing, for he suddenly shook his head and stepped back. Sarah could not stop an expression of regret from flitting across her face.

"We're going to hunt on foot." His voice was a little rougher than usual. "I'll protect you. We'll clear around the front gates; that's where most of them will be."

"I understand."

Sarah tucked the Walther into her jacket pocket and gripped the shotgun. Grimalkin loped beside her, ever watchful. Silver-lined clouds scudded across the sky, and the night wind tugged at their clothes and ruffled their hair. Sarah found herself smiling and then grinning, like a little girl staying up late on an outing.

"How did we drive out of the estate? There's a wall all the way around." Sarah glanced back at the car and the stretch of wall behind it.

"It's a twist in reality. Don't ask me for details. It allows you to leave the estate, it's part of the escape plan. When we're done hunting you'll have to drive in the front as you normally would."

"My father could twist reality?"

"I doubt it. It was probably set up when the house was built."

They walked on in silence, Sarah wondering just how her magical family had gone undetected by the world at large. She decided to visit the library tomorrow, and see what clues she could pick up.

As they came within sight of the front gate, Sarah could see quite a few sets of glowing eyes and lumbering shapes in the dark. Beside her, the vampire cracked his knuckles.

"What do we do?" asked Sarah, deferring to Grimalkin in matters of combat.

"You go wherever you like, shoot whatever you feel like, and I'll protect you," he replied breezily.

"Right." Sarah set her jaw.

With a whoop, Sarah fired her shotgun. Another creature fell twitching. It had only been a few minutes since the battle had been joined, but Sarah was beginning to feel like an old pro already. Her shots were nervous and careful at first, but Grimalkin's excitement was infectious. The fact that the flesh and bone of the creatures melted into piles of shiny beads and old feathers reassured her also.

Since the creatures were presumably inedible Grimalkin contented himself with using his fists to attack. As she had ordered, he killed them quickly, but nevertheless seemed to take great enjoyment in their destruction. Sarah realized just how cruel it had been to lock him up in that deserted house for all those years. It was getting more and more difficult to believe he had deserved it.

He absorbed any blows aimed at her and returned them with interest. He was capable of punching right through ribcages and snapping bones like they were chalk. *And he's mine.* Sarah exulted in their power. She stopped and reloaded, her faithful guardian keeping watch.

"Now you understand," his words were low and warm, and Sarah glowed to hear the pride in them.

"It is kind of fun, once you get used to it," she smiled.

"We're nearly done here. The fun will be over soon." He did sound disappointed.

"There will be other nights."

The expression on his face was indescribable, a mixture of relief, hope, joy, and something darker that made her weak at the knees.

"Master," he murmured fervently. He turned abruptly and faced the darkness, as if he could no longer trust himself to look at her. Sarah bit her lip.

The last creature lumbered mindlessly towards its fate, unaware of the competition for its life. Laughing, master and slave dashed towards it, vying for the honor of killing the last monster. Sarah was quite sure that Grimalkin was deliberately slowing for her, but was having too much fun to care. They were nearly upon the beast when she sensed Grimalkin tense to spring. She fired her shotgun from the hip, and let her momentum carry her forward a few steps as it fell. Grimalkin put his foot through its skull, just to make sure it was dead.

"I got it!" Sarah yelled triumphantly. She knew her hair was tangled and she probably reeked of gunpowder, but she felt absolutely and almost absurdly strong and happy.

"You're beautiful." Grimalkin's eyes widened in surprise, as if the words had slipped out unbidden. Sarah stared at him, her mouth open in shock. Unnoticed beside them, the corpse collapsed into a pile of sparkly paper and bits of glass.

Sarah knew the words were genuine; the look of surprise that gave way to one of trepidation could not have been faked. Her heart thumped in her breast, and she felt as if her stomach held butterflies the size of cats.

He stepped closer; she wasn't going to catch her breath anytime soon. His hands lifted to her shoulders, but did not touch her. His fingers curled on empty air, longing written so plainly across his face it made her ache. Sarah suddenly realized that without permission he could not touch her, no matter how much he might want to.

Sarah took a deep breath and slowly lifted up her hands and placed them on his shoulders, his hair like dark silk under her fingers. His eyes seemed to glow like hot coals; such was the intensity of his stare. He appeared to be holding his breath. Still he did not allow his fingers to so much as brush her fleece-lined jacket.

It was now or never. Sarah could feel her nerve beginning to crack as the adrenaline from the hunt wore off. She could practically see the sensible part of her brain kick itself into gear; diatribe about danger and responsibility fully-formed and ready to drag her back into the boring, everyday, *faded* Sarah that the vampire had teased. She didn't want that. She wanted to see that look on his face more often, the look that said he wanted her, not as a master or as part of his mind games, but as a woman. She pushed herself up and pressed her lips to his.

His lips were cool and soft and he smelled like he had done in her dream, dark and wild. Sarah felt herself go weak at the knees, such was the electricity generated by that simple touch. He appeared to be holding back, letting her take the lead for now, his palms resting lightly on her shoulders.

Her fingers tangled in his hair, and she felt his muscles tighten in his shoulders as he willed himself self-control. She could still back out if she wanted, that was what he was offering her. It was an offer she scorned.

She tasted him. She let her tongue flick over his lips briefly, teasingly. It was enough to snap what little self-control he had left.

Permission granted.

Sarah wasn't prepared for what happened next. His hands slipped from her shoulders to the small of her back, and crushed her against his long, lean frame. His head tilted and he invaded her mouth roughly; tasting, exploring, insatiable. Sarah's knees buckled as she moaned against his mouth.

He supported her weight easily with one arm, while he raised the other and slid his fingers through her hair. Overcoming her initial shock, Sarah returned the kiss fiercely, sliding her hands round the back of his neck. She slid her tongue over his, and boldly flicked it down his long incisors. He made a sound that was almost a purr; a throaty exhalation of desire and delight that fanned the heat between her legs into an inferno. She wanted him. She wanted him like she had wanted no man before him; without restraint or reason. She pushed herself against him, frustrated by the layers of clothing between her heated flesh and his.

Finally she pulled back, nearly dizzy from lack of air. Grimalkin ran a finger over her kiss-swollen lips. The kiss had been so unexpected and intense his thoughts were an incoherent jumble. In his long memory, he could not recall having been caught off guard so completely. Did she know how beautiful and wanton she looked like that? He hadn't been this hard in decades. He was this close to taking her right there under the moon.

Her hands slid down his chest. Her breathing was still ragged, but she managed to get out a single word, "Car."

Grimalkin nodded, and regretfully released her from his embrace. She stumbled slightly and picked up the shotgun. Neither of them had noticed she'd dropped it.

Sarah walked quickly, not daring to look at her companion. Her body was aching for his touch, and she concentrated on putting one foot in front of the other as fast as possible. She stumbled, and instantly his hand was on her arm to steady her. It stayed there.

Finally they came within sight of the car. Grimalkin stepped ahead to open the door for her. Sarah leaned in and threw the shotgun gently onto the back seat. She climbed into the car and wondered if she would have to initiate everything between them.

Instead of walking around to his door, Grimalkin followed Sarah in and she found herself pushed back until she was lying along the seat. Grimalkin leaned back to pull the door closed behind him, then crawled on top of her, his long hair trailing across her cheek. Apparently she didn't have to initiate everything after all.

Chapter 5

Sarah lay back along the seat, the smell of dust, gunpowder, old leather and *him* in her nostrils. It was quite dark in the car, but she could feel his breath on her face, and sense his hands resting on the leather either side of her head.

He shifted above her, one of his knees resting between her legs. Transferring his weight to his left arm, he ran his cool fingers down the side of her face, stroking her neck and letting them come to rest at the zipper of her jacket.

"Lovely," he murmured, and bent his head to once again capture her lips with his own.

Whatever nervousness, or perhaps common sense, had reasserted itself during the walk back to the car, was lost again as the vampire slid his tongue across hers. Gentle at first, his kisses became harder and more demanding as he ran his hand down her side, investigating her curves through the layers of fabric.

Their ragged breathing filled the space as Sarah arched against him, running her fingers down his chest. Her fingers pressed lightly against his lean, hard stomach, only to recoil in surprise as they brushed the head of his cock that pushed against the fabric.

He nipped playfully at her jaw as he unzipped her jacket. Sarah pushed up against his hand eagerly and moved her fingers to his collar to start on the endless row of coat buttons. Grimalkin ran his hand over her breast, feeling the nipple pushing through the cotton fabric of her bra and shirt. He ran his thumb over it, teasing it to greater size and she moaned in his mouth.

Sarah had never done anything as reckless as this since, well, that very morning actually, when she had walked knowingly back into the lair of a vampire. A week ago she would have balked at the idea of making love in a car, let alone to a near-stranger she had only met two days ago. It was no ordinary car, and Grimalkin was certainly no ordinary stranger, and no ordinary man.

The way he made her feel, so free and beautiful, and the way he made her body respond, Sarah thought rather fuzzily through the haze of desire, she might never go back to a living man again. When she was with him there could be no thoughts of anyone else, the idea was impossible. He was so dark, so strong, and so intense. There was no one else in the universe, just them in the cabin of a car, and the slanted stripes of moonlight.

He had undone the first few buttons on her shirt, and he ran his tongue down her neck, lapping at the hollow above her collarbone. He ran one long incisor up her neck, and Sarah felt a thrill of fear. It was a momentary fission, nothing more, for he could no more hurt her than he could pull the moon down from the sky.

He gently but firmly drove his knee up between her legs, and Sarah gasped and saw stars. She wanted him now; she ached for release from her core, why the hell did he have to wear so many clothes? She started on the buttons on his shirt in a fever of impatience.

Still she felt uneasy; something was nagging at her, trying to get her attention through the fog of passion that clouded her thoughts. Something she should really consider before going any further. Suddenly she sat up so fast she cracked her forehead against Grimalkin's nose. The vampire recoiled in shock.

"What?!" His look of surprise was almost comical.

"What about the creatures?" Sarah looked up at him with wide, worried eyes. Grimalkin blinked at her, puzzled. "The creatures, we cleared them out around here and around the entrance. Could there be more?"

Her words seemed to have finally gotten through, for the vampire heaved a frustrated sigh. "Yes," he eventually admitted, rather resentfully.

"We can't..." to her annoyance, Sarah felt her cheeks begin to burn, "do this here," she finished, rather lamely.

"You're right of course," Grimalkin nodded, and backed off her.

Immediately she was regretful of the loss of his presence. Her body screamed at her in frustration as she slid herself into the driver's seat. Grimalkin reached back and reattached the wire he'd disconnected earlier. Sarah fit the key in the ignition, not bothering to do up the buttons on her shirt.

Grimalkin sprawled in his seat, his coat open and his shirt unbuttoned to just below the line of his pectoral muscles. He made no attempt to hide the fact that he was still hard. Instead he watched her. To Sarah's infinite disappointment, his trademark smile hovered around his lips.

The ride back was spent in rather strained silence. The tension between them was palpable, but not as friendly as before. Grimalkin hated himself for it, but he found himself feeling resentful towards her. So close, and yet so far, but what rankled him the most was the fact that she was right. He had let nearly two decades of sexual frustration blind him to danger, and it was she, the human, the one he was supposed to protect who had called attention to his oversight.

It had been so wonderful to see her fight, to see her share his dark delight in battle. It induced an unfamiliar feeling; happiness perhaps. How absurd; he'd always been happy. Fate had handed him a beautiful gift, an endless life of joy. And endless darkness, of course, but that was a small price to pay, and he paid it gladly. And endless hunger. Grimalkin blinked in surprise as the realization hit him; for the all too brief time he had spent in her arms, the tide of his dark thirst had receded. All he had wanted, all he had needed, was her. *What are you doing to me, how are you doing this?* he wondered in quiet despair, for centuries of habit and old instincts were kicking in. However delightful it had been to be caught so thoroughly by surprise, he was regaining his composure. The man was turning back into the fiend, and the fiend sought to best its master by any means.

Sarah sensed something of the thoughts that were occupying her companion. His eyes were still alight with desire, but his old amused reserve was returning. She was on trial again, and the thought was enough to make tears prick at her eyes. *Why the hell did he have to be this way? Couldn't they continue as they were, uninhibited and warm?* She shook her head; she shouldn't have expected this to be easy. He wasn't even human, how could she expect to touch his heart? Even assuming he had one.

She glanced over at him briefly, meeting his eyes for one short, troubled second. No, she thought, he did have a heart in there somewhere. What had happened between them earlier had been real. She had glimpsed it before, underneath all the vicious smiles and arrogance; a despair that he probably didn't know he had. His look when she had left the previous evening had spoken volumes. He was nothing without her; inconsequential and alone. No wonder he wanted to dominate her.

Sarah felt her heart swell with pity for the vampire, but she was careful not to let it show. He would not appreciate it, she knew. Sarah was in over her head; the sensible thing would be to leave. She looked at him again; he had transferred his attention to the moonlit scenery outside, presenting her with his dark profile.

She couldn't leave, not without trying to get back that warmth. It was so small and so perfect; like a tiny flower growing between them, and so fragile. This, she felt, was worth taking some chances for.

"We are so incomplete," she murmured sadly. If he heard her he showed no sign.

They arrived at the second pair of gates, Sarah's station wagon still where she'd left it, and she drove around it carefully. Grimalkin stirred.

"I can put the car away."

"Please do." Sarah tossed him the keys and walked back to the house, her hands shoved deep in her pockets.

The question was; what to do now? Her body still ached for his touch, and their previous...adventures had upped the stakes in their little power play considerably. If she went back to town he would see her as running away and any respect she had gained tonight would be lost. If she stayed...she knew what would happen; their chemistry could not be denied. She must remain in control, but her body and her emotions were treacherous. Her nipples were tightening at the mere thought of resuming what she had so dramatically halted. He had who knew how many centuries of experience to draw on. But she was the master. Sarah smiled and her stomach clenched in nervous anticipation. Could she, dare she?

"I need a whip," she said with nervous humor.

"What for?"

She jumped in surprise; he moved too quietly. He was leaning against the doorframe, his clothing still in delightful disarray. His mouth was curved into an arrogant smirk, and his eyes gleamed with triumph and not a little lust.

Sarah took a deep breath and stiffened her spine. You're the boss, she told herself. If only he was more convinced of that fact, maybe she could believe it. Sarah never scored above a B in drama at high school, but at that moment she would have made Miss Wright proud. She smiled faintly and strode from the room, her head high. Slightly puzzled, but still certain of his victory, Grimalkin ambled after her.

Sarah's heart was hammering in her chest and her palms were damp. She hadn't been this nervous since her first statewide competition. Her competitor this time was much more intimidating. She heard the deep voice of the vampire behind her.

"You need to relax. I won't bite--this time."

Anger flared, burning away some of the nerves. "No, you certainly won't." Her voice was so cold she barely recognized it as her own. The surprise she had induced was palpable, and she resisted the urge to look back and gloat.

Instead of going up to the master bedroom, Sarah turned into one of the drawing rooms and, with a flourish, pulled the dustcover off an old armchair. She turned and dropped into the chair, crossing her legs and resting her hands imperiously on the armrests. She looked up at Grimalkin, her eyes blazing.

To her relief, the vampire was looking rather nonplussed by her behavior. If he had still appeared to be in control her nerve would have cracked. Not wishing to lose momentum, she waved her hand authoritatively.

"It's too dark in here."

Too surprised to argue, Grimalkin walked over and turned on a lamp, and warm light spilled across the carpeted floor. Sarah continued to stare straight ahead, willing herself courage and control.

"Master," he began.

"Don't talk," she ordered, neatly forestalling any verbal attempt he might make to regain control of the situation. "Stand in front of me."

He did so, and Sarah felt a thrill run through her. However thoughtful or gentle they had been, the men in Sarah's life had always taken control. Having such a powerful man obey her every command wasn't merely enjoyable, Sarah was beginning to find it exciting. Unconsciously she pressed her thighs together, squeezing the heat between her legs.

Grimalkin noticed this and attempted to reclaim control, letting a knowing smile grace his lips, and looking her up and down slowly, undressing and devouring her with his eyes. Sarah didn't blush or look away; her carnal instincts had been denied once too often. Her breathing shallow and her eyes slightly glazed, she was going to get what she wanted. On her terms.

She looked the vampire up and down, her tongue flicking out over her lower lip. Grimalkin tried to be angry, but found he was beginning to enjoy himself, noticeably and almost painfully. He was getting a taste for the unexpected, it seemed. Her gaze flicked down, and he saw her legs tense again. Grimalkin was surprised, slightly embarrassed, and incredibly turned on.

"Take off your clothes." Her voice was deep and husky. Grimalkin's hand traveled to his shirt almost immediately, but then he changed his mind and sat on a footstool, slowly unlacing his boots. Sarah's burning gaze not missing a movement of his nimble fingers.

He stood up again, his feet bare. Sarah watched him shrug off his coat and place it neatly over the back of a chair. His crimson eyes met hers as he began to undo the rest of the buttons on his creamy white shirt. Sarah was pleased to note that he seemed to be enjoying giving his performance. He was an exhibitionist at heart, and loved showing off, she knew. He let the shirt fall from his shoulders to the floor.

The lamplight highlighted the muscles that rolled under his skin as he moved to pick up the shirt and toss it over his coat. His torso was lean, the muscles defined but not bulky, and a trail of fine dark hair traced a line from his chest to his belt. Sarah stared with unfeigned admiration and lust. He was beautiful and, as he moved, he showed that he knew it.

He began to undo his belt.

Sarah's fingers twitched as the last of his clothing fell to the floor. Whatever inhibitions still held her back, fell away with the last piece of fabric. He stood before her, proud and strong, desire tensing every muscle of his long frame. She regarded, frankly and appreciatively, the steel length that stood proudly from the dark tangle.

She hadn't planned any further than this, but some part of her, long neglected and suppressed, had taken over. Sarah knew what she wanted, whether she admitted it to herself or not.

"Play with yourself." The words shocked her, even though she had uttered them.

"What?" However surprised she was, it was nothing compared to the astonishment reflected on Grimalkin's face.

"I told you not to speak," she reprimanded him. "Very well, don't do anything." Her eyes narrowed in mischief.

She began to undo the rest of her buttons. His expression was frankly greedy as she reached back to undo the clasp on her bra. She smiled; he should have realized this was a punishment, not a reward. She brushed her tight and aching nipples and Grimalkin's jaw went slack, his eyes glued to her fingers. She relished the way his heated gaze stroked her; never had she held a man's attention so effortlessly and completely. He was all hers.

"Take off my boots." He didn't need to be told twice. "Keep kneeling." He looked up at her as she stood in front of him and shimmied out of her jeans and underwear. She sat back down again, her legs slightly parted.

"It's a shame you're so inhibited," she said mockingly as her hand slid over her breasts and down her stomach to the nest of pale gold curls.

The muscles in his jaw jumped as he restrained himself from saying anything. Sarah nearly lifted the restriction on speaking just to hear him beg, but decided she had done teasing. Instead she leant forward and pulled his head towards her.

"I think that's enough punishment." Her voice was ragged and breathy. He bent his dark head to her. "Oh, fuck!" She threw her head back as his long tongue rubbed against her sensitive core.

He lapped at her eagerly, her thighs resting on his broad shoulders. He really did like showing off. Sarah whimpered and gasped, incapable of doing more than tangling her fingers weakly in his long hair. She felt his muscles move as he stroked himself, his breathing ragged. His long tongue explored and skillfully teased her until the feeling was so intense she nearly gasped for him to stop. She could feel her orgasm building, almost painfully slowly.

She felt as if her entire being had contracted down into a single point of pleasure, her mind and personality lost in a sea of light. Dimly she felt the vampire shudder beneath her and she fell, his name on her lips as she came. Grimalkin continued his ministrations until, gasping and shaking, she gently pushed him away.

The vampire sat back, his head resting on the arm of the chair, and a wry, self-deprecating smile on his lips. "It seems I underestimated you, Master."

"Uh-huh." Sarah didn't feel up to forming coherent sentences yet. She sat back and looked at her slave though half-closed eyes. Peaceful silence descended, and Sarah could feel herself drifting off. With a sigh she roused herself and started sleepily pulling on her clothes.

Grimalkin got dressed in record time, and was waiting fully clothed by the time Sarah was fumbling drowsily with the buttons on her shirt. Pulling on her boots she cracked a yawn so wide it brought tears to the corner of her eyes.

Grimalkin was strangely silent, and Sarah was too tired to initiate a conversation. The tables had been turned successfully, and she wanted to sleep. She walked back to the kitchen to collect her bag.

"You're not leaving are you?"

Sarah suppressed a smile at the almost hurt tone of Grimalkin's voice. She collected her bag and swept out the front door. "Well of course I am. It's..." she checked her watch, "past two am. With one thing and another I'm exhausted. I'm going back to the motel for some sleep."

"But you could stay here."

"Grimalkin, everything's covered in dust-sheets, and I'm certainly not going to go hunting for linen at this time of the morning. Besides," Sarah decided to turn the screws a little to make up for earlier, "I don't particularly want you hovering beside my bed."

"I wouldn't do that." Grimalkin's long legs easily matched her pace as she trotted to her car.

She looked up at him warily, the moonlight reflecting off her pale hair but shadows obscuring her eyes. "Wouldn't you?" She couldn't keep the bitterness from her tone.

Grimalkin bowed his head, his long hair falling in front of his eyes, and was silent.

He rested his forehead against the cold bars of the gate and watched her taillights wink out as she rounded a curve in the long driveway. It was probably safe enough for now, but he took little comfort at the thought.

"You got what you wanted, didn't you?" he snarled at himself. The evening was a success, surely; he had induced her to hunt and kill and he had seen her trembling and calling out his name as she came. He had been in half a mind to seduce her all along, to turn her into something like himself, so the years of slavery that stretched ahead of him would not be so constricting. But she had bested him, somehow taken everything he'd thrown at her and turned it around. And she had driven off, stronger perhaps, but just as human as when she had arrived.

He let his anger build, his awareness expanding until he could sense every warm-blooded movement on the estate, from the tiniest mouse to the stag that had lived in the woods for a few years now. He let the thirst take over, pushing aside for now the confusing emotions that slowed him down and made him weak. All he needed was the hunt, to become the hunt. Whatever strange and forgotten sides of him his master was unearthing, this was immutable; this was stone. *I am, therefore I hunt. I hunt, therefore I am.*

With a growl, the predator leapt easily onto one of the gargoyles that flanked the iron gate, gulping hungrily of the cold night air. Until he turned his blood-smeared face to the eastern sky stained with sun he could pretend he was free.

Sarah awoke to bright sunlight streaming in though lace curtains and the smell of muffins drifting up from the floor below. It wasn't until she was halfway through combing her hair in front of the vanity mirror in her room that she remembered why she was so tired. She stared into her own eyes as a blush crept right to the roots of her pale hair. *Oh my god what was I thinking?* She buried her face in her hands out of sheer embarrassment. *I haven't been acting like myself at all*, she thought, *but it's much too early for menopause. What am I doing?* Still, she couldn't keep a satisfied smirk off her face as the memory of the previous night came into focus. She reminded herself that he only objected when she had tried to leave.

Her spirits fell as she remembered their less than pleasant parting. She supposed she'd have to patch things up after the sun set; she was becoming quite proud of her vampire management skills. She looked at herself in the mirror, and practiced a commanding look.

"I am now Sarah, Vampire Tamer!" She collapsed into giggles. "I should call Rebecca, she'll never believe it. *Now* who's the one to brag about having a gorgeous, well... he's not really a boyfriend is he?"

Ignoring her protesting stomach, Sarah sat down and dialed her friend's number. To her disappointment, it appeared Rebecca wasn't home. Since it was too early to be at work, Sarah supposed she wasn't the only one with a new...companion. Sarah left a cryptic message on her friend's phone and headed down for breakfast.

As she had planned the night before, Sarah went to the public library, settling herself down in one of the slightly musty overstuffed chairs with some books of local history.

As she had expected, her family had settled in the area a long time ago; the big house had gone up before the town hall. The Berkley name cropped up fairly frequently in Armstead's history; her ancestors had held positions on the local council and had helped to finance a few of the public buildings, including the library that Sarah was now in. Nothing seemed out of the ordinary, to Sarah's disappointment.

On impulse, Sarah pulled down a dictionary and flipped through it until she reached the g's. She ran her finger over the page.

"Grimalkin: old she-cat, spiteful old woman." She felt herself smile, "Not the most flattering moniker, Grimalkin." Next to the entry someone had scrawled in pencil one word: *why?* "That's what I'd like to know," Sarah murmured.

Sarah went and asked the librarian where she might obtain information from past issues of the local newspaper, and was guided into a small room with a microfiche. It appeared computers were yet to invade the sleepy town. Gathering up her courage, Sarah pulled up the issues from exactly twelve years ago, and began going through them methodically, starting in January.

She was halfway through August when she came across a death notice considered so important by the editor it made the front page. It announced the death of Michael Andrew Berkley, who had succumbed after a mercifully brief fight with lung cancer. A few days later the funeral was covered in full. Sarah sat frozen in shock, for there was a large picture of the funeral and mourners, and featured prominently among them a young girl, her face wary and grave.

Sarah stared back at her own face, feeling hot tears well up uncontrollably. The girl was surrounded by people, but she looked so lost and alone, her worried gaze fixed on something outside the frame of the photograph. Sarah took deep breaths, trying to calm herself, and turned her attention to the other mourners in the picture. She half-expected to see Grimalkin's face among the solemn gathering, but there was no sign of the vampire.

There was one face she recognized. A small, worried looking man, his face half turned away from the camera, stood at the edge of the mourners. Despite the fact that the library was warm, Sarah shivered, and an icy fear clutched her heart. Her heart pounding, Sarah searched the caption for the man's name, but it appeared he was one of the 'and mourners'.

Sarah sat back from the machine and rubbed her eyes. Did she really have to dig up all this history? The man might not still be alive, let alone in the area. Sarah felt that the newspaper told the truth when it described her father's death as natural. Why should she torment herself when there was nothing to be gained? It wasn't as if she didn't have enough on her plate already. She thought about trying to find her mother's death notice, but realized with a rather sad shock that she didn't know which year her mother died. The information would be back at the house, presumably in the papers Grimalkin claimed were locked away somewhere. Sarah thought about the size of the house's underground complex and decided it might be better to wait and let the vampire show her, as opposed to blundering about herself. She didn't want to faint again. She was so deep in thought that she didn't hear the stranger approach.

"Miss Berkley?"

Chapter 6

Sarah jumped and spun the chair around, her eyes wide with fright. Standing in the doorway was a man around her age wearing a light business suit and a pair of gold-rimmed glasses.

"I'm sorry, I didn't mean to startle you." He smiled benignly.

"Oh...uhh...that's all right, I was just reading. Who are you?"

"Jonathan Berkley." He smiled at her obvious shock and held out his hand.

Sarah shook it warily.

"I'm your cousin, but I don't believe we've ever met before. It's such a pleasure to meet you."

"Likewise." Sarah did not sound very sincere, but he appeared not to notice her suspicion.

"I own a modest stretch of land on the other side of town, so please feel free to visit any time. Wait, I know, you haven't been properly welcomed back yet. How about Friday night? Just a little gathering, meet the locals, that sort of thing. I know there are quite a few people dying to meet you."

"Uhh, Mr. Berkley-"

"John, please. We're family now, Sarah. And I insist. We Berkleys must stick together. I look forward to becoming friends with you." He blinked and rubbed his forehead and Sarah suddenly realized how nervous he was. She smiled in relief; her thoughts had been on vampires and monsters for too long. It hadn't occurred to her that merely approaching a long lost relative could be such a nerve-wracking experience. It was a nice reminder that there were ordinary people in the world, ordinary Berkleys. She wondered if John knew anything of the Berkley secrets and duty.

"Would you like to go out for some lunch?" His voice broke into her thoughts.

She smiled politely and turned off the microfiche, keeping her body between her cousin and the screen. Relative or not, her business was her own, and she didn't want him asking awkward questions.

"So you've seen the main house?" They had adjourned to a small café near the library and Sarah had ordered yet more coffee and a chicken salad.

"I've been up there a couple times. It's sadly neglected."

"I wanted to keep it in good condition, but your father's will stipulated that it be left pretty much as you see it now until you returned. It was a most peculiar will."

"Did you know my father?"

"I might have seen him once or twice, but my father and yours weren't very close. So, have you met the monster?"

"Monster?" Sarah was instantly on her guard.

John laughed. "It's just a local legend that there's a vicious monster that guards Berkley Manor." He waved his hand. "It's just local superstition. There's nothing to fear, Sarah."

"Ah." Sarah smiled weakly and busied herself with her salad.

"So you will come on Friday? For the party."

"It's a party now? I really don't have any suitable clothes-"

"You really aren't used to money are you? Just buy some, or have some made. It's no big deal."

"Oh, right." He obviously had no idea how involved buying a new dress could be.

"Anyway, just turn up anytime after seven. My house is here." He drew a quick sketch on a napkin and handed it to her. "So tell me, what have you been doing all these years?"

John appeared to listen intently as Sarah detailed the story of her life after her father's death. Sarah didn't think it was that interesting, but John appeared to be hanging on to every word. He seemed genuinely interested in her career as a pistol shooter, and Sarah enjoyed the opportunity to ramble on in fine detail about her favorite pastime. The worries of the past few days vanished as Sarah discussed barrel length and trigger weights to her attentive audience.

Before she knew it, it was mid afternoon. The sight of the shadows lengthening across the road made her gut clench with foreboding. Instinctively she glanced towards the house, although she couldn't see more than the shops across the street.

"You know, I'd better be going," she said distantly.

John looked disappointed. "Are you sure? It's been really nice getting to know you."

"Well, I have to call my friend back in the city; she should be getting home from work soon. I haven't told her about the inheritance yet," Sarah said, reaching for her handbag. The lie slipped out easily and naturally.

"Ah, yes of course. Don't worry, I'll pay the bill."

"Thank you." Sarah was already halfway towards the door. The feeling that something was wrong just wouldn't go away.

"Don't forget, Friday at seven," he called after her.

The bed and breakfast where Sarah was staying was within walking distance, but it seemed an agonizingly long way away as Sarah trotted down the street, her hair swinging behind her. The sense of looming disaster was visceral and urgent. The smiles that Sarah received from the locals seemed distant and distorted, as if viewed from underwater. She had spent the afternoon in the daylight world, but even though the sun still shone Sarah knew she had entered the other side of reality. Here there were monsters.

Sarah swung past the hotel gate and made straight for her car. She was fumbling for her keys before she was even halfway across the small parking lot.

Pausing only briefly to check that she still had her pistol and that it was loaded, Sarah drove away with a screech of tires. Driving in such a manner that only two weeks ago would have caused her to close her eyes and scream, she tore along the country roads to her estate.

It might not have been rational to behave in such a way over a mere gut feeling, but Sarah had left rationality behind long ago. She smiled grimly and thought briefly that it had been quite easy to pick up 'the Berkley paranoia'.

The gate was locked. Sarah almost cried with relief, but still couldn't shake the feeling that something was wrong. She stopped and listened. The trees rustled softly and, somewhere in the distance, was the grumbling purr of a tractor. Nothing seemed amiss. Sarah got out her semiautomatic and wondered if she should have kept hold of the supernaturally modified weapons. Too late now.

Sarah's shoes crunched on the gravel as her senses strained to work out what was wrong. It wasn't until she reached the step that she noticed that the front door was slightly ajar. Sarah knew that Grimalkin would never be so careless as to leave it open. She adjusted the grip on her pistol and nudged the door open. Thankfully it didn't creak.

The feeling when one's home has been occupied by uninvited guests is an uncomfortable one, prickly and animal. The manor wasn't exactly Sarah's home, but the hairs on the back of her neck rose and she felt queasy as she noticed small signs of disturbance. The house had been quickly and professionally searched.

It appeared that the searchers were gone. There was an air of vacancy, and there had been no cars at the gate.

"The armory," Sarah breathed. Losing some of her caution she turned and walked hastily down the remembered stairs. She ran up to the steel door and pushed hard. To her relief it was still locked, although there were some scratches that testified that an attempt had been made to break in.

"I thought this place was supposed to be protected," Sarah muttered angrily to herself. "And where is the protector? Grimalkin!" she called. The sense of catastrophe returned like a punch in the gut. Sarah called again, this time more urgently. The house was eerily silent.

Sarah summoned what courage she could and set out in search of him, her pistol gripped so tightly her knuckles whitened. She turned to go deeper into the underground complex and then halted.

"No, aboveground," she murmured. How she knew this she couldn't tell, but her instincts had been serving her well today, and she wasn't about to abandon them. She called again and started opening doors in a whirl of frustrated worry.

"Grimalkin!" The kitchen and storerooms were empty. "If the intruders came in the front door he should be near the entrance." Sarah retraced her steps, tearing open doors along the way.

"Grimalkin, where are you? Upstairs? No." Sarah's instinct kicked her towards a pair of ornate doors that she knew led to what was once a grand dining hall, now standing empty.

Sarah shoved the doors open so hard they rebounded off the walls with a bang. She skidded forward on the hardwood floor. There were a series of large windows along the western side of the room, and sunlight slanted through wooden blinds, tiger-striping the area. He was here, she knew.

"Grimalkin, where...?" She trailed off as her brain finally processed what her eyes were telling her. Grimalkin was on his knees in the center of the room, and his head was tilted back, as if he were staring at the ceiling. Sarah stepped forward hesitantly.

"Gri...Grimalkin?" There was something strange about his posture, something stiff and unnatural. "Oh, my God." The gun fell from Sarah's nerveless fingers, clattering unheeded to the floor. A heavy silver cross, at least a foot long, had been driven through Grimalkin's throat, between his collarbones and into his chest.

"Grim." Sarah's vision swam as she blinked away tears. "Who did this to you?" Sarah crossed the few feet separating them and stared down into his face. His eyes, now a dull red, gazed sightlessly at the ceiling, and not a muscle in his face twitched. Sarah's fingers curled nervously as she hovered over him for a second.

Screwing up her courage, Sarah wrapped her fingers around the arms of the cross. She pulled gently, not wanting to hurt the vampire any more than he already had been, but it refused to budge. Gritting her teeth, she pulled as hard as she could, but only caused his frame to rock slightly.

"I'm sorry about this, Grim." Sarah placed one foot on his shoulder to brace herself and *pulled*. There was a distressing sucking sound and the cross came free. Sarah overbalanced and fell to the ground, the cross skidding away from her across the floor.

She sat up quickly and peered hopefully into Grimalkin's eyes, but they were as vacant as before. She tried not to look at the gaping hole in his throat but noticed that very little blood oozed from it.

"Blood, of course. You need blood to mend yourself. Hold on, Grim, I'll find something." Sarah dashed towards the kitchen and was staring blankly at the cupboard before she realized how senseless that was. "Animals, rats..." Sarah looked about wildly, a note of hysteria in her mumblings. Her eye fell on the rack of knives. She halted, her breath rasping in her throat; she looked down at her hands and noticed that they were shaking. She swallowed.

"Blood. Right. No problem, I can do this." She gingerly reached up and pulled a knife from the rack. She looked at it for a moment before running back to the dining room.

Grimalkin hadn't moved by the time she returned. Sarah sat down on the floor and gently pulled him back until his head rested on her lap.

"Please let this work." Sarah heard her voice crack and her vision swam again. She cuffed the tears away from her eyes and laid the blade against her arm. "Don't want to hit a major artery or vein, so just a small cut." Sarah wished that she had more than a vague idea as to where the major arteries and veins were. She took a deep breath, and with her face screwed up in expectation, ran the edge along her arm.

The blade was sharp, and almost immediately red blood began to well from the wound. Sarah tilted Grimalkin's head back and with her other hand gently pried his jaws apart a little way. She held her arm above him and watched as the liquid dripped into his mouth. Nothing happened.

Sarah stayed like that as the last rays of light retreated up the eastern wall. She couldn't bear to look at the man in her arms; instead she closed her eyes and tried to swallow her tears.

"You said...you were really hard to kill. So, so you have to wake up, Grim. You have to," she sniffled. The cut on her arm stung, but it was nothing compared to the pain in her heart.

Sarah jumped as something lightly brushed her arm. The room had grown quite dark, and Sarah looked down as the feeling came again. He was licking her arm. His eyes were unfocused, but there was life in them. Sarah stared at him, a wave of relief pushing the air from her lungs.

"Delicious," he whispered, and his lips pulled back from his fangs.

Sarah pulled her arm away; she didn't want to be bitten. Grimalkin blinked and shifted his gaze to her white and drawn face.

He still seemed rather out of it. "There is nothing better than awakening with your blood on my lips."

Sarah couldn't suppress a shudder. "Are you all right?" She helped him sit up.

He shook his head rather dazedly. "It'll take more than that to kill me, Master." His voice was gaining strength with each word, and Sarah sensed the undercurrent of anger. "Although it's a good thing they didn't think to open the blinds."

Sarah's thoughts, however, were not on revenge. She hardly dared believe he could have healed such a horrible wound so fast. She crept around to face him and cautiously glanced at his throat. There was no wound, just pale, unblemished skin.

"Thank goodness," Sarah sobbed, and launched herself into his arms.

Grimalkin's mouth dropped open in shock as Sarah sobbed into his coat. Instinctively he wrapped his arms around her and pressed his cheek against her hair.

"I was so scared." Her voice was muffled by tears and cloth. "I thought they'd killed you. And I'd been so mean to you last night; I'd not gotten to say I was sorry."

"Sorry? For what? I deserved it." In truth, until the intruders had arrived he had spent the day feeling guilty. Not so much for what he had done, but for what he had wanted and had attempted to do. He had behaved terribly, and now she was crying against his chest because she was worried about him. He knew he didn't deserve this kind of compassion, but now that he had it, by the gods he was never going to let it go. "Sarah."

She pulled away slightly at the sound of her name. Grimalkin cupped her cheek and gently turned her face up towards him. Her eyes and nose were red from crying and he wiped away a stray tear with his thumb.

"These are...for me?" He couldn't keep the wonder from his voice. She merely nodded. He looked down into her face, and felt a strange tightness in his throat that wasn't from the injury. "You are really something," was all he could manage to say. He might have said more, but his senses could no longer be ignored. He inhaled deeply. "Fresh blood?"

Sarah held up her arm. The cut had started to scab over, but her sudden movement had opened it again.

Grimalkin inhaled sharply. "You silly girl. You didn't need to go that far. I...I thought that was just a dream."

"I thought you were dying," Sarah said faintly as she examined the wound a bit incredulously.

Grimalkin ran his hand over his face as he fought the instinct to sink his fangs into her arm. "There should be a first aid kit in the kitchen." He stood up and gently pulled her to her feet, carefully not looking at her arm.

"Is it that bad?" she asked.

"No," he sighed. "Even if I tried anything the charms would stop me, physically if necessary. But it's not...pleasant." He shot a quick, rueful smile at her and strode ahead to the kitchen.

"You don't have to. I can do it," Sarah protested as he took down a box from high in a cupboard.

"It will be quicker if I do it. Here, wash the worst of it off." Grimalkin pulled her towards the sink.

"Are you sure you don't want to-"

"Don't tempt me, woman!" he snarled furiously then looked away, angered at his momentary loss of control. "Just wash it off," he muttered, and started rummaging through the box.

Sarah recoiled and then silently did as she was bid.

"I don't think it needs stitches, so I'll just clean it and bandage it. This box is pretty old, but this should still be good." He held up a dark glass bottle and turned back to the sink.

"Will it hurt?" Sarah asked anxiously.

"Probably," he replied. "Just try to think of something else." He bent down until his mouth was next to her ear. "Like the fun we had last night, perhaps."

Sarah turned, the retort on her lips transforming into a pained hiss as he poured the stuff over her arm.

Grimalkin was quick and efficient, and this prompted Sarah to ask where he had acquired his experience.

"I studied to be a doctor in the late nineteenth century, sort of. I apprenticed myself to a drunken old fool in East London for a while. He didn't seem to notice that I was only around after dark."

"Why?"

"I needed to disappear from the vampire community for a while, so I found a profession that required spending time with lots of people who were probably going to die anyway."

"That's horrible," Sarah exclaimed.

"Actually I believe 'natural selection' is the technical term." Grimalkin grinned at her.

Sarah absently fingered the neat bandage on her forearm. "Thank you," she said quietly.

"You're welcome." Grimalkin put the box back where he found it. "You seem rather subdued."

"Are we safe? I thought this place was supposed to be protected."

Grimalkin frowned thoughtfully. "It's a mystery to me as well; how they got in. Either they were invited or they've got some powerful wizards on-side."

"I haven't invited anyone. Which reminds me, I'm supposed to go to a party on Friday."

"Party?" Grimalkin raised an eyebrow. "Is that safe?"

"I don't know. I met my cousin today, or at least, someone claiming to be my cousin."

"Did you think he was lying?"

"No."

"Then he probably is your cousin. I gather there are branches of the Berkley family all over the place; a sort of back up plan, should the main branch be wiped out."

"That's not reassuring; he didn't seem very intimidating."

"It's surprising how much ordinary people can change, once they find out about things," the vampire smirked.

"What's that supposed to mean?"

"Oh, nothing. Anyway, if you want to go to the party, then go." Grimalkin stood before her, his arms crossed proudly over his chest. "After nightfall nothing can hurt you, for I shall stand in their way."

"It's good to see you're back to normal," Sarah grinned. "Anyway, I might transfer my stuff from the motel."

"Really? You're moving in here?" Grimalkin couldn't keep the eagerness out of his voice.

"I think it will be safer." Sarah stood and headed for the front door.

"True," Grimalkin nodded wisely. "Wait, safer for whom?"

Sarah's laughter rang down the hall. "Well, who was the one who got hurt?"

Grimalkin tried to work up a frown, but it slid into a grin. She was coming to stay with him. Of her own free will. He sauntered along after her and wondered what else she might do of her own free will.

"Okay, here we are." Sarah flicked on the light switch and tossed her handbag onto the small table near the door.

Grimalkin hadn't said much during the ride to the motel; his attention had been glued to the scenery outside. *He should hate me*, Sarah thought. *He's been locked away from the world for almost as long as I've been alive.* But he didn't hate her. He didn't even seem to hate her father, although his true feelings on that topic were obscure. *That's the way he is*, Sarah realized suddenly, *he doesn't see things in terms of wrong or right.* Her father did what he had to do and Grimalkin had made his peace with that, during those long years in the dark.

"That's really very impressive," she said out loud with a smile.

Grimalkin blinked at her in surprise. "Are you referring to last night?" He grinned broadly.

Sarah laughed easily--she was laughing more often nowadays--but a shade of meaning now hung between them, thickening the air and imbuing movements and glances with a new significance.

He was so incongruous, standing in the middle of her small hotel room, his archaic clothes and long hair contrasting with the bright and cheerful décor. He looked around with interest.

"Is that a television?" he pointed. "They've really improved." He carefully wasn't meeting her eyes.

Sarah giggled. "Do you want to see what's on?"

He nodded eagerly and she tossed him the remote. Sarah went into the bathroom to start packing, listening to the vampire channel surfing in the next room.

Sarah bent down to check that she hadn't left anything in the cupboard under the basin only to yelp in surprise as she stood up again. Reflected in the bathroom mirror, she could see the vampire leaning against the doorframe, just watching her.

"You- you reflect in the mirror." Sarah glanced behind her.

"How do you think I keep looking this good?" he smirked.

Sarah glanced back at the vampire with a frown. "You're out of synch with your reflection."

"They don't always work perfectly," he shrugged. His eyes darkened. "I'm sure you don't find it *that* interesting."

"Actually...uhh..." Sarah trailed off as Grimalkin stepped closer, never breaking eye contact, until he was mere inches from her. His presence made the room feel tiny. Sarah's heart began to thump and she swallowed nervously as her stomach clenched in anticipation.

Grimalkin bent forward until his mouth was next to her ear. He could sense the way her heart beat faster and it delighted him. She was like a little bird in the palm of his hand, warm and fluttery- no, not anymore. Under his influence she was becoming a hunting hawk, and she was all the more attractive for it. Now he had to coax her to fly.

"Sarah," his voice was as dark as mahogany, "tell me to step away and I will. I deserve nothing better." He pulled back to look into her eyes. "Master, tell me, what do you truly want? Tell me I can..." he leant in until their lips almost touched, "kiss you."

Sarah could barely breathe. Her knees were weak, and she was supporting herself by leaning against the basin behind her. She wanted him with an intensity that was almost painful. To feel his skin against her own, to entangle herself in him, to take him inside her, nothing else mattered. And he hadn't even touched her.

There were no excuses. She was no longer under the spell and exhilaration of the hunt. There was just him. Just him and her and the fire that was so easily kindled between them. Sarah knew that once she gave permission there would be no going back, no giving orders. It was no simple kiss he asked for, it was a symbol of the temporary removal of the wall between them.

Sarah tilted her head slightly. "Yes," she breathed against his mouth.

Chapter 7

A smile ghosted across his lips, and then he kissed her. It was a deep kiss, slow and heated, banking the fire that consumed them both. Sarah leant into it, losing herself in the sensation. His long arms wound around her, gently but firmly pulling her against him. Sarah was unresisting in his embrace; everything just felt so right.

His hands slid down her back and cupped her buttocks through the denim of her jeans. Sarah jumped and tried to pull away slightly, but the vampire tightened his grip, his kiss almost bruising in its intensity. She could feel his cock pushing against her stomach and her insides clenched in response. Sarah begged the universe that there would be no interruptions this time. Perhaps the universe heard her.

With a growl, Grimalkin pushed her back until she bumped into the tiled wall between the shower recess and the mirror. With only a smothered squeak of protest, Sarah realized he wasn't even going to let them adjourn to the bedroom next door.

His hands slid around across her belly and his long fingers hooked into the waistband of her jeans. In a fever of impatience he pushed her shirt up, his fingers skimming over her smooth skin until he reached her bra. Grimalkin pulled away slightly and looked at her, his crimson eyes burning with lust, his lips slightly parted. Sarah gave a wicked little smile and reached down to caress his length through his clothes. He exhaled raggedly and then with one swift movement pushed her bra and shirt up over her breasts.

The clothing was uncomfortable bunched up across her chest, and so Sarah released her gentle grip on his cock and held her arms above her head. Obediently Grimalkin started pulling her shirt and bra up over her head. Her vision obscured by the cloth, Sarah jumped as she felt Grimalkin lap at the valley between her breasts. Goosebumps rippled across her skin at the shock and she heard the vampire give a breathy chuckle. She was about to voice a complaint when he pulled the offending fabric from around her head and tossed it carelessly behind him.

Sarah grabbed his face in her hands and pulled him into another kiss, nibbling at his lower lip. His tongue flicked across her lips as he reached around her and crushed her against him again.

Sarah felt almost despairing as she started on the buttons on his coat, but to her surprise the garment practically fell away, and the shirt soon followed, joining the pile of clothes on the cold tiled floor.

The vampire bent his head to kiss and lick and nip at the sensitive flesh of her neck and collarbone. Sarah shivered in delight and, for the first time, allowed her hands to glide over his chest, her fingernails gently scraping at his flat nipples.

He made that purring sound again. God, it was sexy, Sarah thought, and she heard herself moan in response. Grimalkin hooked his fingers into the waistband of her jeans, sliding them around until they met at the button. Sarah knew what was coming next, and so she kicked off her shoes, thankful that she hadn't worn her boots. To her surprise, Grimalkin just stepped out of his boots and kicked them away. Her thoughts were on other parts of his anatomy, but she did wonder how he did it.

In a hurried whirl of fingers and cloth and buttons, the rest of their clothes were discarded. Sarah shrieked as he pushed her against the wall again, the tiles a cold surprise against her back and ass. Grimalkin chuckled again and pushed himself up against her. Hard, smooth, soft, rough, cool, oh god, she could feel him with her entire body as she pushed against him. Sarah was suddenly grateful for the cool wall as a wave of heat rolled over her, making her heart race and her breath catch in her throat.

Grimalkin gently drove his knee up between her legs. His long, cool fingers stroked her hips, moving to slide down her thighs. All this time he kissed her, sliding his tongue across hers as her hands fisted and tangled in his hair.

He drew her knees up, and she trusted him with her weight, wrapping her legs around his hips and crossing her ankles. He braced her against the wall, but in his strong arms she had no fear of falling. Her only thought, her only desire, was to feel him inside her, to bring herself to release. He was only too happy to oblige.

He pulled away from their fevered kiss to look at her with half-closed eyes, dark with lust. She could see the question in his eyes as the head of his cock nuzzled against her. Her mouth fell open as he pushed a bit more impatiently.

"Please," she managed to rasp out. "Grimalkin, just..." Her words dissolved into an ecstatic moan as he slowly ground his hips up to hers.

It had been close to twenty years since he had held a woman this way. The way she accepted him, held him, ground and thrust herself against him- it took all of his willpower not to try and sink his fangs into her. Instead he buried himself in her, slaking his aching, roaring lust as if he were human.

Hot and sweaty she moaned and gasped in his ear, her legs tensing around his hips, urging him deeper, harder. It was an expression of life the likes of which Grimalkin could not remember experiencing before.

Already her movements were becoming more insistent and uncoordinated and her breathy moans filled the confined space. Grimalkin felt her nails dig into his shoulders as she came with such force it seemed to tear the breath from her lungs. He held himself back, just a few seconds more, devouring and savoring, every breath, every movement; making this moment of her his to keep forever.

She barely had time to draw breath when he pressed them against the wall one last time with a ragged moan, his body tensed; his arms like bands of steel around her. With a sigh he gently lowered her until her feet could touch the floor again. Her knees buckled.

He changed his grip and picked her up again, carrying her to the bed in the next room. His duty done, he crawled in tiredly beside her.

He was hoping she would snuggle up against him; he was getting used to her warmth, but instead she wrapped her arms around a pillow and looked at him. Oh yes, she was becoming a strong master. His plans of domination seemed so stupid now.

"Not bad for a dead guy." She broke into his thoughts.

"Not bad? Is that all you can say?" he asked, mock-affronted. She laughed; a bubbling, pleasant sound that he wanted to hear again.

She looked thoughtful for a moment. "Grimalkin, how do I know that the house is safe?"

"Well, the defenses appear to be-"

"No, that's not what I meant. I mean now, I just somehow *know* that the house is still safe. And...I knew you were hurt, back in town, I knew." Her voice was becoming more strained as she went on.

"Don't worry." He tried to calm her down, and wished he could hold her again. "I wouldn't surprise me if you had some kind of power. I told you your family was strange. It wouldn't surprise me if previous Berkley's married things not quite human."

"What?"

"I'd imagine it would be a lonely life. You can't just tell anybody the truth, so a person who already knew..."

"So I'm psychic?"

"Probably. Don't force it or rush it, you'll get used to it. You're a very strong woman, Master."

They lapsed into silence for a while. "I see. I can't share or explain this to anyone until what? ...our wedding night?"

Grimalkin's jaw tightened in instinctive fury at the thought. *She's not marrying anyone! If she tries I'll*...of course he couldn't do anything. But still, not an hour after they were entangled in the bathroom and she's already imagining marrying someone else, someone human?

"I don't know," he said finally.

"Well, we have more immediate problems."

"Master, you know that I will be by your side forever."

"I also know that's because you don't have a choice." She shook her head. "Anyway, moving on. I saw my picture today, in the newspaper." Grimalkin listened attentively, but said nothing. "And I saw someone else. I don't know, I can't remember, but he made me scared. A small guy, worried face."

"Thinning hair and glasses?" the vampire asked.

"Yes! How did you know?"

"You don't remember do you, what happened after your father died? I suppose...I didn't want to tell you this. You should find out for yourself, but I don't want you to suffer either. As always, I can only tell you what I know.

"I was alone in the dark, and then someone opened my door. And there was blood, sweet and dark on the floor. It woke me, and I desired to taste more of it, but I did not know the extent of the magic that still bound me. There was a little girl, injured and frightened, she asked for my help. I realized who she was, who you were, Master. There were men chasing her, after the Berkley collection I suppose. There was a man there like you described, but he kept to the back of the fray. I was very weak, but I fought them. There was much death, much blood. Master...should I stop?"

Tears were streaming down Sarah's face as she stared off into the distance. She shivered.

"Please, Master, I'm sorry. Let me hold you, I-"

"No, Grimalkin. You said I was strong, but I need to be stronger. I just...so that's where the nightmares came from. That man...why didn't you kill him?"

"Because you were injured and scared and begged me not to go."

"So it was you I found, there in the dark." She pushed some strands of hair out of her face. "No wonder I was scared. What happened? Why didn't anyone know of this?"

"Well, I knew you weren't going to stay and be my master at that age. And I didn't want you sent to jail or wherever. So I asked you if you would let me hide the bodies."

"So they're still there?"

"Buried in the estate. I can show you if you'd like."

"I...I still... Why don't I remember this?" She looked at him pleadingly.

"Because you're not ready to accept the past. The person you were then and the person you are now are still separate. When you are whole again, then you will truly be the master. Your portrait will hang in the hall."

"The painting?"

"It's centuries old. I don't know the story, but it was originally a self-portrait by one of your more gifted ancestors. *The Master of the Hunt.* It will change to reflect who the current master is. At the moment the estate is still, magically speaking, your father's. Perhaps that is why the outer defenses were breached today."

"So I have to remember."

"I don't think that's the root of the problem. Master, do not worry, this will come in time."

"Speaking of time, we still have to move my stuff over to the house."

"Of course." Grimalkin stood and walked into the bathroom, returning momentarily fully-dressed and carrying Sarah's clothes.

"How do you *do* that?" she demanded.

"This?" Grimalkin asked, opening his coat slightly. "I've been stuck in your basement for nearly twenty years. The rats don't provide a laundry service. This outfit was made in Vienna a couple centuries ago. It'll last as long as I do, and requires no more than a thought to put on."

"I don't suppose this tailor is still around? I could use a wardrobe like that."

The gun jumped twice in quick succession as Sarah emptied the magazine for the tenth time that afternoon. With relief, she pulled off her ear-muffs and ran her fingers though her hair. She still couldn't connect, couldn't remember anything of the story that Grimalkin had told her, but it was beginning to become a compulsion, to become the Berkley master in more but name. And so, for the three days since she had moved to her manor, Sarah would set up some targets behind the house and practice her sharp shooting. She would practice until dusk, when Grimalkin would emerge from the house and help her pack away her guns.

Although she had caught the vampire looking at her lustfully a few times, they had not been intimate since that night in the motel room. Sarah wasn't sure quite what their relationship was anymore, although Grimalkin seemed quite happy to be used as a sex toy, should she desire it.

Since that night the vampire appeared to be more at peace with himself. He still teased her, but it was gentler banter, almost affectionate. It was that affection that Sarah was scared of. It was only beginning to sink in that he was hers for the rest of her life, and Sarah worried about the kind of twisted relationship that could spring from their strange bond. She still had to remind herself that he wasn't human, even when she'd seen him lope back to the house with his chin smeared with blood and his eyes bright.

Sarah picked up her gun case and wondered where her slave was. He'd usually be here by now, enquiring as to how her day had been and scenting the air for warm creatures. She carried her guns back to the armory, which was becoming her favorite place in the house, all the while keeping an eye out for the vampire.

"Master." Sarah jumped, and Grimalkin smiled, looking pleased that he'd snuck up on her. "I've found it." With a flourish he held up an evening gown of dark blue-gray silk.

"What's that? Where did you get it?" Sarah tried to be irritated, but she couldn't help but eye the garment covetously.

"From the attic," he replied promptly. "I've been looking for something suitable for you to wear to this party your comparatively unattractive cousin is holding."

"And who appointed you guardian of my wardrobe? You're not related to a Rebecca by any chance?" she asked suspiciously.

"Master, I have observed the most attractive and fashionable ladies of more eras than I would care to count, so believe me when I say that with this you will outshine them all."

Sarah raised an eyebrow. "I don't think I could outshine anyone. Still, I'd forgotten all about that wretched party. And..." she ran her hand lightly over the fabric, "it doesn't look too bad."

"Go on, show me." He held it out.

Sarah shrugged and gingerly took the gown. "Are there many gowns up there?"

"A few. Not all are in as good condition as this one, though."

Sarah gave a cynical little smile. "So it's just a coincidence that the best one happens to match your outfit?"

"You weren't planning on going alone, were you?"

"Well, I don't want my cousin to know about you."

"I won't bite anyone," he promised, then amended. "Without due cause."

Sarah sighed. "I'm not saying I don't want you around, I just don't want you visible. And for some reason I have the idea that you'd be a terrible show-off given a chance like this."

"Me, Master? Never."

Sarah just shook her head and left to change.

She hadn't liked the dress. Grimalkin was sure it was a mixture of low self-esteem and contrariness, but in the end she couldn't be bothered with finding an alternative. When Friday had finally rolled around she had retreated to the master bathroom muttering evilly about 'flat, limp, hair'. They had agreed that he wasn't to show himself at her cousin's house unless she was in trouble. Grimalkin waited patiently near the foot of the stairs in the entrance hall and concocted different definitions of 'trouble'.

The last few days had been difficult for Grimalkin. He could deal with the frustration of having her sleep in the same house, yet so far from him. He could deal with the smell of gunpowder and of cooking. He was even beginning to enjoy taking orders.

What was disconcerting was the warmth he felt inside whenever she was near. The way her voice lingered in his head long after they spoke, the way she seemed to insinuate herself effortlessly into every plan, every daydream, every lustful reverie, every reflective moment. It had taken him the best part of a week, but Grimalkin finally had to admit it to himself. He'd fallen in love with her. And this time, he felt, it would take centuries to get over it.

To compound his problems, it appeared she didn't feel the same. He sensed her desire sometimes, but always she held herself back. *She* remembered the difference between them, the gap between living and dead, predator and prey, master and slave. So she had shared her body and nothing more. Her strength sometimes angered him, and yet it was part of what he loved about her.

While dwelling on these thoughts often led him to rage or melancholy, when he stopped and just existed with her, when he thought of her walking in the sun above him, or sleeping in the house he protected, he felt quietly, impossibly, happy. And that's all that mattered; he decided he would be happy to be her slave, forever. He would accompany her, a protective shadow, wherever she would go. And if she should find another, then...he would be protected, too, Grimalkin decided eventually, although the vampire reserved the right to get rid of anyone obviously unsuitable.

"Well?" She appeared at the top of the stairs, her hair pulled up in a complicated bun and the gown shimmering over her curves.

Grimalkin looked up at her and felt his jaw drop.

"I know it's not that good," she said, while fiddling with her purse.

"It's magnificent. You're magnificent." He held out his hand for her, "You outshine your mother in that dress." He brought himself up short and gulped.

Sarah's eyes narrowed. "You knew my mother? You've never mentioned it before," she said sharply, suspicion coloring her words.

"Well, I only saw her once; I can't say I knew her."

She was not convinced. Mistrust knotted in her stomach like a cold, grey stone. "Where did you meet my mother?"

"Madrid."

"What were you doing there? What was she doing there?"

"I was doing what I always do--existing. She was there with your father on one of his expeditions."

"You're hiding something," Sarah stated. "Tell me what."

"Your mother had her own career. She was a hunter. I told you the vampire families tried to get rid of me; they put a bounty on my head. Your mother came to collect."

"You...you killed my mother!" Sarah grasped the banister for support as she stared at the vampire.

"No!" Grimalkin barked indignantly. "At least, not directly," he added in a mutter.

"Tell me everything." Her voice was like cracking ice.

"Your mother and I fought. She was injured and I escaped. I...I don't know if it lead to her death. I know she died almost a year and a half later, but I believe it was from an illness."

"That's why my father hunted you." Sarah nodded to herself.

"His love for your mother gave him the strength of thousands. I've never fought someone as stubborn, brave or just plain determined. No matter what I did, or who I threatened, he just kept coming."

Sarah glanced over at the portrait. "He...he was a great man."

"And your mother was more than a match for him. She didn't look much like you, but she was very beautiful and brave. I've never seen anyone handle a shotgun like her. She blew me away, literally."

"And yet you don't hate my parents." She looked at him, as if trying to read the answers off his face.

"I couldn't. I was envious, if anything. If it was for her he would, and could, do anything. It takes something powerful for that to happen. I wasn't fettered; I had all my power at my disposal. It was like a force of nature, impossible to hate. Besides, if I held grudges I'd be miserable; I don't want to spend my time doing things I dislike."

"You're...very happy with what you are, aren't you?"

"Yes. My unlife is a gift. I love this world, for all its faults, and I couldn't bear to leave it. Mortals have my pity."

"What if we don't need your pity? What if it's worth it, seeing the sunlight, living amongst friends; what if it's worth dying for that?"

"Then I'm happy for you," he replied shortly. "But don't think you can *ever* make me feel guilty for what I am."

They were face to face now, studying each other's expressions intently. "I'm not trying to make you feel guilty; I'm trying to understand you."

"Until you become like me, I can't see that ever happening."

"Why are you suddenly so angry?"

Grimalkin stepped away, a stubborn expression on his face. "Look, just never mind. I don't like being analyzed like this; let's just go to this pointless party."

"You're jealous of them, aren't you?" Sarah asked wonderingly. "My parents--you want what they had."

"I wouldn't have if I hadn't met you!" He turned on her with a snarl, his teeth bared.

Sarah recoiled, more from the implications of his statement that his fierce posture. Sarah's mouth went dry, and for the first time she saw his eyes hold something approaching dangerously close to hate.

"I don't want this...indignity of being your slave. But I know, if I were free, I would tear you open, devour you completely. I...this is what I am, this is what I would do."

"You mean you wouldn't have any choice?"

"Despite being higher on the food chain, we vampires are...baser creatures. It takes long practice to deny our instincts, practice I certainly haven't had." Suddenly his anger melted away, and he gave a self-deprecating shrug. "It's probably good for me to be taken down a peg or two anyway. Besides, there are compensations." He grinned. "I get to almost take the most beautiful woman to the ball."

"Grimalkin..." Sarah trailed off, a strange mix of emotions coursing through her. She had no words, even if she knew what she wanted to say. He's growing a heart, she thought, and it must hurt like hell.

She looked back at the portrait of her father. To know of her parents' love, it was strangely comforting. As for Grimalkin's admission, it made sense, and she couldn't help but feel pride that her mother had almost taken the vampire down. She believed, or decided to believe, that he had had nothing to do with her mother's death. There was nothing to be gained by worrying about something she would never know the truth of. Besides, justice had already been served; those years of captivity, and possible decades of servitude were probably the worst punishment that could be inflicted on the vampire.

Grimalkin offered his arm and Sarah took it as they walked to her car. She glanced sidelong up at him, studying his starlit profile. She remembered the look in his eyes and the anger in his voice when he talked about the 'indignity' of being her slave. Sarah got a strange, sick feeling in her stomach, a kind of premonition of something inevitable, something that would hurt.

Sarah was unused to driving in high heels, so she let Grimalkin drive. His driving skills were obviously a bit rusty, but he seemed to remember them as they went along. He wasn't a butler; she reminded herself, and certainly not a guardian angel. *Although*, she smiled as she thought to herself, *he does a pretty good impression of one sometimes.*

Chapter 8

"Wow." Sarah poked her head out the window to get a better look at her cousin's house. Unlike her crumbling gothic pile, this house was well lit and modern, and the lights lining the driveway hinted at expanses of well-manicured lawns. Sarah eyed the rows of cars that lined the front of the house with trepidation.

"I had no idea he was planning on inviting the whole town," she said ruefully.

"Your family is important around here. Are you sure you don't want me to come with you?"

"Yes, I'm sure. If I need your help I'll ask for it." She got out of the car and smoothed down her dress nervously. "I feel like Cinderella."

Grimalkin shook his head with a grin. "You do know that you're filthy rich, right?"

"It's easy to forget sometimes. Well, wish me luck."

"Luck for what? The last thing I want you to meet is a handsome prince."

"Not much chance of that." She turned and walked towards the house as Grimalkin faded into the shadows.

Sarah felt uncomfortable in the slinky dress and the night air bit into her bare arms. She shivered and walked a little faster, her heels clicking on the brick driveway.

A movement in the shadows caught her eye and she stopped dead, and squinted into the murky dark. She felt gooseflesh rise along her arms--she was being watched. And it wasn't Grimalkin's amused, protective, surveillance either. She hadn't brought a gun, and she cursed herself for her lack of paranoia.

It was only about twenty feet to the front doors. Sarah wavered, trying to decide whether to make a break for the door or to whistle up her vampire. What made her even more uneasy was her sixth sense, or rather, her lack of it. It was getting easier to read places and situations, but here she was coming up with nothing.

Emptiness. Thoughtlessness. Nothing has a hole within the word. Sarah's thoughts circled around the idea of nothing like leaves in a whirlwind.

There was a scrape from behind her and Sarah jumped, startled out of the unnatural reverie. She spun around, a cry on her lips, only to have it smothered by a huge, callused hand.

There was a shout of alarm from somewhere inside the house, but Sarah wasn't going to wait around for help from that direction. She was sure there was more than one assailant. She drove her spiked heel into her captor's foot just as hard as she could and at the same time sunk her teeth into his hand.

She was too light to make much of an impression with her foot, but her assailant grunted and his grip on her relaxed for an instant. Sarah threw her head back and managed to call out.

"Grim!" Another pair of hands clamped down on her face. Sarah's struggles became wilder as she kicked at everything within reach.

"Get her feet. Ow!" She felt a rush of triumph as her left knee connected with the original attacker's upper thigh.

"A girl's being attacked!" a female shrieked from the direction of the house.

"Leave her alone," breathed a voice right next to her ear. The words were small and quiet compared to the mountain of rage Sarah sensed behind them. She hadn't heard or felt him approach, but he was here. Grimalkin.

The attackers began to release Sarah to deal with this new threat, but they weren't fast enough for the vampire. He brought his arm down and knocked one off his feet as if he were a rag doll. He grabbed the other by the arm and twisted it viciously; the man's jaw went slack from pain as Sarah scrambled away.

"Don't kill them!" she screamed as she caught a glimpse of Grimalkin's face, his lips drawn back in an inhuman snarl. His red eyes narrowed momentarily, and then with one seemingly effortless movement, he ripped the man's right arm off.

"Stay back, I'll deal with this!"

Sarah vaguely recognized her cousin's voice from the house. But she paid it no mind. Instead she fell to her knees, sickened at the sight of Grimalkin holding the gushing limb above his mouth, drinking the gore that stained his face, hands, and coat.

The double doors at the front of the house burst open and her cousin raced out, brandishing a rifle. He stopped dead at the sight of the vampire, who tossed the limb aside and regarded the newcomer without comment or enthusiasm.

Sarah shakily got to her feet, trying to work out how to explain the gory mess, preferably without landing anyone in jail or an asylum.

"Uhh, John, calm down. No one's dead...exactly. I was attacked and..." She trailed off as her hands started to shake uncontrollably. Another man had followed her cousin out of the house; a short man, with thinning hair and dark, sharp eyes that glittered behind a pair of glasses.

"Y-you." Her eyes were wide with shock and fear. Grimalkin strode over to stand beside her, his crimson gaze hard and cold.

"What's going on here?" John looked about as sick as Sarah felt. "That man needs a doctor-" He looked around wildly, as if one might materialize from the darkness.

"*I'm* a doctor," the short man behind him said mildly. "I think everyone should go back inside now." He waved his hand and John blinked and headed uncertainly for the door. "Except you of course, Miss Berkley."

Sarah took a deep breath and kicked off her heels. She didn't know what was going to happen, but her shoes were only going to slow her down. John hovered in the doorway, still looking shell-shocked; she knew she wasn't going to get any help from that direction.

Grimalkin stepped in front of her, his blood-splattered face twisted into a mad smile. Sarah sensed the energy in him, like a dog pulling on the end of a leash.

"Who are you?" she called over Grimalkin's shoulder.

"Me? You mean you don't know? Ah, that's right. You didn't remember much, if I recall. I am Doctor Hegerty, a one-time employee of the Berkley family."

"I didn't get to kill you last time," Grimalkin growled. "I won't make the same mistake twice."

"But will *she*?"

"Huh?" Grimalkin's hands clenched and unclenched. He seemed to be scanning the area for more enemies.

"Well, Sarah? How do you like playing the necromancer? It's quite a rush, isn't it?"

"I'm not a necromancer." Sarah watched Hegerty closely, wondering why he didn't seem afraid of the vampire.

"Oh, yes, you are, my dear. You are controlling an abomination, an undead monster. If that's not necromancy I don't know what is. Did you really think that all this came without price? The blood that drips from your creature's jaws...it should be on you."

The man with one arm groaned and clutched at his shoulder; he was presumably only semi-conscious.

"That is your doing. That is a human being who lies bleeding to death there."

"He attacked me!" Sarah protested indignantly.

"Master, tell me I can kill him now." Grimalkin glanced back angrily over his shoulder. "He has nothing useful to say."

"Just try it, beast." He turned his attention back to Sarah. "I don't want to hurt you, Sarah. I just think that you are...unsuited to the task your father left for you. This world will corrupt you; turn you into a monster like *him*." He pointed accusingly at Grimalkin, who was still impatiently switching his attention from the doctor to Sarah.

"My father wasn't corrupt." Sarah folded her arms across her chest.

"No, no," he replied, his hands held up in a placatory gesture, "but he had the advantage of being trained for twenty years by your grandfather. You, Sarah, are an ordinary young woman who doesn't deserve all this darkness and death thrust upon her."

"Sarah, don't listen to him. He was with the men who tried to kill you when you were just a girl."

"Yes, I was there. I was trying to protect you Sarah, but I am a weak man, unable to do much but watch in horror, and when I knew you were physically safe, I left."

"Liar!" Grimalkin spat. "Let me kill him."

"I don't remember what happened," Sarah said quietly, "but I trust my instincts."

"He'll manipulate them!" Hegerty interjected.

"And my instincts say you're lying," Sarah finished evenly. She turned and nodded once at Grimalkin, who grinned like a maniac.

"Come on then, doctor," he said mockingly, "let's see what you've got!"

He didn't wait for a reply. He practically flew up the driveway, his fingers curled and clawing at the cold night air, his dark hair streaming out behind him. Sarah braced herself for the bloody end to what appeared to be a one-sided fight.

Grimalkin stopped. It was as if he'd run into an invisible wall. His hair and coat whipped about him as he tried to hold his ground. Sarah saw his boots skidding on the bricks. Hegerty just gave a sharp little smile, his eyes glinting behind his glasses.

Grimalkin leapt. Effortlessly, he rose at least fifteen feet into the air. He arched his body mid-flight and dove down at his adversary, his fangs bared. Hegerty made a sweeping gesture and Grimalkin smashed head first into the driveway, the vampire blown off course like a leaf in the wind.

Sarah flinched as her guardian was driven into the ground hard enough to crack the mortar between the stylishly patterned bricks. He lay still for a second, then with a grunt his limbs twitched and he started to lever himself off the ground.

"Grim! Are you all right?" Sarah started towards the vampire.

"Of course he his." Hegerty's voice was harsh from his exertions. "He's practically indestructible, if the stories are true. But attacking me is just a waste of energy."

"Not," Grimalkin staggered to his feet, the bloody cracks in his skull healing as he spoke, "if you give me more power, my master."

"Power?"

He nodded. "Release some of the bindings upon me, and I will obliterate this insect from the face of the earth."

"Now do you see, Sarah?" the doctor asked. "You will have to give up your control. He will be bound less and less...and all the crimes he can and *will* commit are your crimes. Do you really think you can control someone so old and powerful forever? He desires it; freedom. He hates you, Sarah. Everything he does, he does to get back control."

"Not true..." Grimalkin mumbled.

"Which bit is not true?" Sarah demanded.

"I don't hate you." He didn't look at her.

"I see. Doctor Hegerty, what is it that you want with me?"

Grimalkin looked at her, his eyes pleading.

"I know I'm not a Berkley, but John is. He'd be much more suitable to take care of the collection. You needn't give up anything else; your money is your own."

"You think you can control him." She nodded to herself. "Well, some things are a little more important than my soul, or even the fate of these wretched thugs." Sarah drew herself up to her full height and took a deep breath, her hands clenched by her sides. "Grimalkin, how do I release your powers?"

Grimalkin didn't reply, instead he leapt in front of Sarah. He grunted as something slammed into his chest. As before, he began to be pushed back. Sarah bumped against his back and started shuffling backwards, his coat battering about her legs. Her eye fell on one of the fallen thugs and she blanched. His skin was bubbling and charring, and the most sickening smell began to permeate the air. There was a cracking sound as the windshield on a nearby car fractured. Sarah huddled against the vampire's broad back.

"What do I do?" she yelled. Even the air seemed brittle; every blade of grass, every leaf was straining, unnaturally still, as if assailed by huge pressure on all sides.

"I...hereby release..." Grimalkin gritted out, "vampiric powers...until the enemy lies dead." His boots were skidding on the ground and Sarah stumbled backwards. "Sarah!" He half turned as he heard her fall and Sarah smelt ozone as the air in front of him began to ionize.

"Ihearbyreleaseyourvampiricpowersuntiltheenemyliesdead!" Sarah shrieked, instinctively covering her head with her hands as the pent-up energy began to stream around him, turning the planes of his face a glowing white.

The pressure dissipated. The ground itself seemed to shiver with relief. Sarah felt the air agitate, and heard the trees begin to toss their branches angrily. Wisps of blond hair escaped from her bun and she brushed them out of her face and looked up.

Grimalkin stood above her like a god of death. Sarah could sense his aura of power, like a dark miasma swirling and clouding about him. The night itself curled and twisted upon itself to do his bidding. He tilted his head up and looked at the star-splattered sky with the reverence of a worshipper in a temple.

She saw him as he truly was; old and as powerful as the night itself. The veneer of humanity stripped and cracked from him, leaving something beautiful and alien. Sarah felt something warm on her face and realized she was crying. The sense of joy, the sense of release and truth--his emotions were so huge they spilled over. Sarah felt herself being washed away by him, overwhelmed.

Hegerty looked truly afraid. Still, he did not back down, his hands weaving complicated patterns in the air, and glyphs scoring themselves into the ground at his feet.

"See what you have done!" His voice cracked as he called to Sarah.

Sarah nodded dumbly; she saw, although she could not begin to comprehend.

Grimalkin walked towards the doctor, with the unstoppable determination of a glacier. His feet barely touched the ground, and yet his footsteps resonated like that of a god's. Or a demon's.

He reached the invisible wall again and ran his hand over it. The air rippled. He drew his arm back and *punched.* There was a crack like thunder and the vampire's arm went through Hegerty's defenses. Hegerty made a chopping motion with his arm and Grimalkin's wrist snapped downwards, his hand hanging limply. Hegerty pressed home his advantage. Grimalkin continued to smile as invisible hands snapped his neck. Hegerty didn't stop there. He poured his power into the destruction of the vampire, snapping and shattering his bones again and again. Finally he stopped, falling to his knees in exhaustion.

"I...I did it," he said wonderingly.

"I doubt that." Sarah got to her feet, rather shakily. "Grimalkin, get up and finish him."

"You silly girl, I-"

"Yes, Master." The shattered remains of the vampire began to collect themselves as the doctor looked on in horror.

Sarah could only describe him as coagulating, such was the damage done to his frame. Within seconds, Grimalkin was on his feet, looming over Hegerty with an expression of great anticipation.

"Miss Berkley, Sarah, you can still save me. I'll go away, I'll do anything," the doctor begged.

Sarah's lip curled. "I don't think so. Grimalkin, do as you will."

She didn't stay to watch. Instead she picked up her shoes and began to walk to the car. Something in her mind was stirring, dark memories of dust and blood and stone paving. She heard a gurgling scream from behind her, but didn't look around.

Like an automaton, she found the keys Grimalkin had left in the car. Without thinking, she started the engine and carefully pulled away. Grimalkin would follow when he was ready, she knew. With the doctor dead or dying, his powers would be resealed, and he would return to her side. Her beautiful, abominable slave.

Sarah sat in the kitchen and waited for him. Her hairdo was looking worse for wear, and her makeup was smeared but she paid such small distractions no mind. She was beginning to see what she had to do.

When Grimalkin returned he looked as immaculate and laid-back as always. He swept into the room with an extravagant bow and complimented her on her performance.

"I did what I had to do," she said. "That's what being a Berkley means."

"Well, yes," he replied cautiously, "but that doesn't mean you can't have fun doing it."

"That was your idea of fun?" she snapped at him, then instantly regretted it. "I'm sorry. You can't help being what you are."

"Master," he stepped forward, "those things he said; they weren't me. I am happy here, with you."

"Maybe. But you can't hide from me the happiness you felt when I unsealed you. I had no idea you were so powerful."

"Well," he struck a pose, "I am rather impressive, if I do say so myself."

She rolled her eyes. "What else can I expect from an egomaniac?" She got to her feet. "Anyway, we have to finish this. I have to remember."

"What are we doing?"

"We're going downstairs. We're going to find that room where this all began."

"You mean my room?"

"You still live in the same room?" She looked at him incredulously.

"Well, why not?"

"Because you were sealed up in there. Doesn't that bother you?"

"No," he answered truthfully.

"What happened after I left?" Sarah asked a short time later, as she led the way down into the basement complex.

"Your cousin was trying to calm the other guests down, I gather. I don't think anyone saw much. I disposed of the doctor and dumped those worthless men outside the local hospital."

"They're alive?"

"You told me not to kill them. So I didn't."

"But you ripped his arm off!"

"And strangely enough, his blood coagulated to an almost supernatural degree, thereby saving his life." He grinned wickedly.

Sarah sighed and shook her head. "Anyway, here we are." They had arrived at the corridor where Sarah had collapsed that afternoon not so long ago.

"What are you going to do?" Grimalkin asked, looking at her with a hint of worry in his eyes.

"I'm going to walk down here. I'm going to try and remember." She turned and looked back at him. "Catch me if I fall?"

"Always."

She walked forward, the flagstones cold under her feet, just as they were when...

Sarah didn't really understand what the will meant exactly, she just knew the second the lawyer had finished talking, that she'd done something terribly, terribly wrong. Her uncle, a pale man with a moustache like a caterpillar, glared at her with such venom it made the twelve-year-old sick.

Father was gone, and the enormity of the loss overwhelmed her. She wanted to scream wordlessly at the sky, to curl up in a ball and die, to run away until she couldn't remember even having a father in the first place. Instead she sat quietly, fidgeting in her good dress, listening to the adults talk and watching the back of her uncle's head and feeling icy tendrils of pure fear wrap around her heart.

She knew her family was not like other families. They had a duty, and she was studying and learning so that someday she, too, would take on that duty. Now...she didn't know what would happen to her. She didn't want to leave, but she couldn't stay in the house all by herself, could she? She hoped she wouldn't have to stay with her uncle.

The lawyer eventually left, and Sarah wondered who all these strange men were. She assumed they were with the lawyer; but why were they still here? She slipped away from the group, some instinct leading her back to the study. She could hear her uncle talking with another man, a small, worried man she had assumed was a clerk of some description.

"...Can we really do that though? Surely it's rather risky."

"You are a Berkley. The laws of the land, or even of nature, do not always apply to you. You should have studied your family history better--succession by assassination is practically a family tradition."

"She's just a girl."

"Who has been trained since birth by Michael. The will was carefully crafted to cut you out of the family business and you know it. Are we just going to take this lying down?"

"We? I don't like you, Hegerty...yet, you have a point." Her uncle's voice shook with anger. "How dare he? Leaving everything to a child! He wasn't right in the head--can we contest the will?"

"You said yourself that some things must be kept within the family. It's your choice, of course."

"All right. Where is she?"

"Right outside the door," Hegerty replied smugly.

Sarah felt herself go cold. She was so quiet, how had he known? She didn't wait to find out. She turned and ran. The familiar curves and corners of her house now took on malevolent hooks and edges, snagging at her skirt as she pelted away from the study in a blind panic.

She crawled into one of the cupboards and huddled behind a box of cleaning stuff. Her heart was beating so loudly that she was sure the entire country could hear it. How had he known she was there? She bit back a squeak of fear as heavy, male footsteps went past her hiding place.

He'd known she was hiding behind the door. She could almost hear her father's voice in her head, that quiet, encouraging tone he'd take when she was working on a particularly hard math problem. He could sense her presence--he knew where she was. Move girl! Her father's voice echoed in her head.

Blinking away tears, Sarah tumbled out of the cupboard to see Hegerty and her uncle at the end of the corridor. Scrambling to her feet, she heard a bang from behind her, and something tore through her calf. She let out a mewl of pain but kept running, even as she felt blood running down her leg and soaking into her sock.

Where? She skidded and turned down another corridor, her breath rasping in her throat. Why hadn't they caught up to her? There was a crash as someone behind her tripped and fell. Her father--he was looking after her still, she realized as fresh tears gathered in the corner of her eyes.

Protected. As if of their own accord, her feet turned down towards the basement. She didn't want to die. She didn't--she stopped and looked around, she hadn't been in this part of the house before; it had always been forbidden to her.

It was behind one of these doors. After her mother had died, her father had gone away for a while. She couldn't really remember it, but she did remember visiting her mother's grave when he had returned.

"When things are at their worst, and you have nowhere else to turn, go to the basement, to the iron door with the big lock. There you will find my last gift to you, and you will be protected."

Sarah limped forward, not daring to examine her leg lest she faint. There were so many doors. Her vision was beginning to blur and she felt lightheaded. Still she kept going, along the endless row of doors, looking for her father's final gift.

There it was. A huge iron lock affixed to a door inscribed with runes. Sarah ran her fingers over the lock and let out a wordless cry of despair--she didn't have a key. I've failed, I've failed, she thought. Goddamn it! Open! She thumped her hand against the door.

It opened. The lock clicked of its own accord and the door swung open silently. Sarah staggered into the room, blinking in the almost total darkness. Something was in here...something dark and dangerous and infinitely more frightening than men with guns.

Sarah turned to run but her legs finally gave out on her. With a cry, she fell to her knees, and immediately wished she hadn't. She sensed something turn its attention to her, its thoughts rolling over her like dark thunderclouds.

"Down here!" A voice echoed weirdly down the corridor. Sarah felt about for a weapon, for anything. Her hand came in contact with something still and cold and dead and she snatched it back, telling herself that whatever it was hadn't moved, hadn't twitched at all.

A light shone into her eyes as her pursuers finally caught up with her.

"She's here--what's that?"

Sarah looked behind her and nearly fainted.

It was a child. It looked barely two years old, and the apparent weakness of its frame was almost obscene when contrasted with the iron chains that bound its tiny form. Maddened, red eyes gleamed briefly as it looked at her before it bent its head forward to the dark liquid that pooled from her leg.

"Part of the collection." She recognized her uncle's voice. "It doesn't look like it's a threat though."

The child was thrown against the wall as one of the men put a bullet in its head for good measure. It made no sound but a brief rattle of chains as they fell from its tiny form. The next bullet was for her, she knew.

She heard the bang and then--nothing. Hesitantly, she opened her eyes--and found herself face to face with a monster. It was still a child, but it had grown appreciably in seconds. Its red eyes gleamed, and its mouth opened to reveal long, pointed teeth and to shape the word, "Master!"

Chapter 9

"Master!"

Sarah found herself face to face with the monster again, his arms wrapped around her tightly. Her heart was racing and her legs felt weak, and for once it wasn't the vampire's proximity that caused it. She wrapped her arms around him and took deep breaths to steady herself.

"You frightened me," she said.

"I was pretty terrifying." He chuckled, the sound reverberating pleasantly through his chest. "You're not frightened of me now, are you Master?"

She remembered the horrifying scene when he fed on the severed arm. The memory still made her nauseated. She considered her reply carefully. "I don't fear you, but I fear what you are capable of."

"And what I am capable of, you have the final say." He shrugged. "So there's nothing to fear."

Sarah couldn't share his lack of concern. Hegerty's words and Grimalkin's temporary transformation were fitting together all too neatly in her mind. Instinctively she hugged him closer.

She sensed rather than saw his pleased surprise at her actions. He pressed himself closer to her, and despite all that had happened that evening, she felt her body respond.

"You know, it is rather a shame. You got all dressed up for nothing." He pulled back and looked at her, tucking a strand of hair behind her ear.

She shrugged. "I didn't really want to go anyway."

"You do look lovely, though."

It was too dark for Sarah to see anything much. The only source of illumination was the indirect glow from the lights in the corridor. Grimalkin was merely a cool, solid shadow.

She shook her head. "I think I'm looking a little worse for wear right now."

"You're entitled to your opinion." He held her hand and swept down into a low bow. "My Lady, may I have this dance?"

"Dance? But there's-"

Sarah felt his other hand snake around her waist and instinctively she put her free hand on his shoulder. "Grimalkin, I can't see a thing. Is this really safe?"

"You're never safer than when you are with me, Sarah. That I promise you."

He pulled her a little closer, and then, to her surprise, the vampire started humming. It started off as a vaguely familiar waltz tune and Grimalkin gently pulled her into the dance.

Even though her eyes were getting accustomed to the gloom, Sarah still wasn't sure where the walls were, or even if there was any furniture in the room. At first she took small, cautious steps, her feet connecting with her dance partner's more than once.

He stopped humming for a moment. "Trust me Sarah, I won't let you hit a wall."

Sarah took a deep breath and closed her eyes. Squinting into the darkness was accomplishing nothing more than distracting her from the dance. And what a dance. Sarah didn't really have a lot of experience, but Grimalkin was the perfect partner, giving her plenty of gentle cues, and he didn't so much as flinch when she trod on his feet.

Eventually Sarah relaxed, and let herself be swept around the room. Her lack of sight heightened her other senses, and her world coalesced into their movement and his humming. His arm had somehow snaked around her waist until she was pulled right up against him. She could feel his coat brushing her through the thin material of the gown. Her bare feet grew so cold they began to feel warm as she unhesitatingly followed his lead in this crazy dance in the dark.

As the dance continued, their steps became less of a waltz and more of a mishmash of whatever Grimalkin felt like doing at that moment. He started humming impromptu, an improvisation of deep, rich tones that ran scales and chased themselves around. Sarah caught snatches of familiar tunes, none remaining true for more than a few bars. It would have been an impossible performance for anyone who actually *had* to breathe.

Her hairstyle was disintegrating even more, and eventually Grimalkin paused and expertly pulled out the pins, letting her pale mane tumble down over her shoulders. He started swinging her around; presumably to appreciate the way her hair went flying behind her.

Sarah stumbled, and rather breathlessly begged him to stop. Her feet were numb with cold and she was starting to feel dizzy. She clung to him to steady herself, laughing in between taking great lungfuls of air.

"You're amazing," she giggled, "if very silly."

"Silly? Whatever do you mean?"

She could feel him smile against her forehead. "I qualified it with 'amazing'. Or does your ego demand more feeding?"

"Always," he laughed.

"How's this then?" On impulse she pushed herself up on her toes and kissed him hard on the mouth.

"Oh, I like that," he mumbled as he kissed her back. "I like that a lot."

He rocked his hips against her so she could feel just how much he liked it. Her hand snaked down and caressed the bulge in his trousers.

"Getting a little ahead of ourselves, aren't we?" she asked teasingly. "I haven't even had dinner yet."

"Well, if you're looking for something to eat..." His voice started off deep and suggestive, only to grow ragged as he trailed off; she was still gently stroking him.

"Is it low-calorie?" she asked seriously. She felt a rush of pride at his surprised chuckle.

"You know, I have no idea. Not," he ran his hand down her side, feeling her warm curves through the thin fabric of the gown, "that a beautiful young thing like you has to worry about calories."

Her skin tingled under his touch, her lack of sight intensifying the sensation. "We can't do this here." She managed to get out, rather breathlessly.

"Can't we? Why not?" His hand caressed the swell of her buttock and then slowly started making its way up again.

"I can't see a thing!"

"You'd like to see a thing?" He chuckled.

"Grimalkin! You know what I mean," she pouted and put her hands on her hips. She felt Grimalkin move as he drew something from his coat. There was a click and suddenly the side of the vampire's face was illuminated.

Sarah blinked at the sudden light. "My flashlight!"

"You left it down here last time you visited." He handed it to her.

Sarah took the instrument and played the light over the room. As she had expected, the walls were plain, unadorned stone. There wasn't any furniture in the room either, at least, nothing resembling any furniture that Sarah had ever seen.

"What's that?" she asked, playing the light over a pile of carefully arranged timber. She walked over and looked into the middle of it. In the centre of the broken bookshelves was a pile of blankets.

"It's...uh, my coffin," Grimalkin said, looking almost embarrassed. "I don't like sleeping without wooden walls around me. It's just a habit I guess."

"It's kind of cute," she said, imagining her big, bad vampire curled up on the pile of blankets. "It's like having a teddy bear."

Grimalkin didn't appear to appreciate the analogy. "Yes, well, if you've finished laughing, let's go upstairs and find you some food."

Sarah grinned. So he was embarrassed enough to forget about sex? He really did have too much pride. She turned and looked at him coquettishly. "Didn't you say you had something for me to eat?"

He stared at her for a spilt-second and then bestowed upon her a seductive smile. "I might have done so," he said in a low tone. "Do you want to go upstairs?"

"No, I think here will be fine," she said, stepping over the barrier onto the blankets. "Ooh, my feet are cold."

Grimalkin watched her scrunch her toes into the fabric. *I can't keep her warm,* he realised sadly, *but I can get her circulation going.* He was a bit surprised, and not a little aroused when she had suggested they stay down in the dungeon. He liked her adventurous side, he was never quite sure what she was going to do next, and while this trait had irritated him at first, now it fascinated him.

He ran his fingers though his hair and kicked off his boots. Last time they had made love with unseemly haste. Now he was going to take his time, employ some of those skills that had, at times, made him marginally famous in certain circles.

He stepped up behind her and lifted her slightly tangled hair to place a soft kiss on the back of her neck. She shivered, and goosebumps rose along her arms. Instinctively she snuggled against him, although he could provide no warmth.

"Master," he whispered.

She gently took hold of his hands and pulled them down around her, relishing the feeling as they slid under her breasts and down her stomach. She sighed as his fingers worked their way through the slit in her dress and caressed her thigh; he was in no hurry.

His hands explored her languidly as he planted hard little kisses along her neck. Sarah was simultaneously relaxed and aroused and she leaned back further against him, carried off by those long, gentle fingers. She barely registered the fact that he'd undone the fastenings on her dress until she felt him step back slightly to ease it off her shoulders to pool at her feet like sparkling cobweb.

"Mmm...hey. Take it off, buddy." She tilted her head back to look at him and hooked her fingers over his collar. "No fair otherwise."

"Since when has either of us been fair?" he chuckled.

It was a fumbling, breathless tumble to the blankets. Hands pushed aside clothes and brushed over smiles in an ungraceful descent to the ground. Sarah snuggled into blankets that smelt of dust and the vampire now shielding her from the cold with his lean body.

Resting his weight on his arms he leant in and pressed his lips to hers gently, his fangs hidden behind the velvet kiss.

"Not too cold?" Her eyelashes fluttered against his cheek.

"You keep me warm," was the whispered reply. Sarah hugged him fiercely, desperately, and he responded in kind.

She could smell him, smell his desire. "Touch me," she murmured, "touch me everywhere. Oh Grim..." Her ferocity and fervour unnerved her as he kissed her again. She wanted to drown in him, be swept away by the magic he wove with his teeth and tongue and hands and cock. She wondered why she suddenly felt like crying. The harder she pushed against him, the more she urged, the slower he went, teasing her, flicking his tongue lightly across her skin like a snake.

"What's the rush? We have all night," he purred next to her ear.

She hitched herself up along him and bumped her head into one of the wooden walls of his 'coffin'. Grimalkin made a wordless sound of sympathy and ceased his ministrations to paw about among the blankets and clothes for the flashlight. Eventually he found the instrument and stood it on its end with the beam pointing at the low stone ceiling. Sarah's previously sightless world coalesced into halftones and vague shapes beyond the immediate illumination.

"Now, where were we?"

"Right here, and you were doing...umm, yes, that."

And effortlessly, they made magic.

Later, after they'd both come, locked in each other's embrace, Sarah had muttered 'more' and she unceremoniously rolled Grimalkin onto his back. The vampire made no comment, but merely watched her ride him, her hair flying and her breasts bouncing with every thrust against him.

When Sarah awoke she was tangled in Grimalkin's blankets and limbs. The vampire barely stirred as she extracted herself from his haphazard embrace. She brushed his hair out of his face and ran her fingers lightly across his lips.

He didn't even twitch; such was the power of the sun, even in this lightless place.

She fished among her clothes for her watch, its luminous dial declaring it relatively early in the morning. She stepped back into her gown, not bothering to straighten it, and padded upstairs for lukewarm shower and a change of clothes.

Sarah stood in front of the portrait in the front room of the mansion, meeting her father's strange, painted gaze. It was still his house.

"What do I have to do?" she asked the mute painting. "Hegerty is dead, I've conquered my fear; I remember what happened now. I--I've agreed. I'll take job, I'll be a Berkley. I'll look after the collection and I'll try to acquire more. What more do I need to do to prove myself?"

But she knew, of course.

Everything she had done, she had done with Grimalkin's help, and while taming him had been a challenge, the real challenge was to face things alone. Grimalkin was only ever supposed to be a last resort--he didn't come as part of the deal, like the house or weapons. He was part of the collection for a reason, although Sarah knew she couldn't bear to lock him away.

She trusted him, but trusting him wasn't enough. She had to trust herself. She had to go it alone.

With her head held high she walked down the now-familiar path to the vampire's lair.

She knelt down beside him and watched him for a while. He barely seemed to breath, and she knew if she rested her head on his chest she would hear no heartbeat, just the hollow sound of his breathing. She clasped her hands in her lap and after several false starts, began to speak.

"Grimalkin, I want to talk to you. Can you hear me?"

With what looked like great effort his eyelids twitched and he managed to mutter, "Daylight."

"I know Grim, I know. But this is the only safe way to do this. I'm really sorry. I've done everything I can think of, but the painting hasn't changed. You said this makes the whole collection more vulnerable--I have to become the master of this house, not just of you."

"No...Master." His words sounded as if they came from a long way away, or from underwater. His hand twitched and he tried to reach for her.

"I can't keep you here, Grim. I felt--I know what you felt when I released your power. You were so happy and free, and I can't keep you locked up like this, even if the cage is gilded. How long have we known each other, Grim? Only a few weeks."

"No, years." His questing hand found her denim-clad knee.

"That doesn't count, Grim. I didn't know you and you didn't know me. Sooner or later you're going to get bored, Grim. You're going to hate me, and call it selfish, but I don't want that."

"Master, it...it's not like that."

"I'm going to trust you, Grimalkin. I'm going to trust you not to come back and try and...claim me or turn me or whatever vampires do. I'm going to trust you not to make me hunt you down for the collection. Because I'd do it, I'd try and kill you. Because I have to, even if it would tear me apart." Sarah blinked back the tears that were stinging her eyes.

Grimalkin didn't say anything, he just looked miserable. Sarah didn't like emotionally blackmailing him in this way, but it was the only way to ensure he behaved once he was out of her power.

"I'm really sorry, Grim. You're the most infuriatingly wonderful man I've ever met, but I know it's not who you are. I don't want something like this to be fake."

"It's not," he pleaded.

"You're not the monster?"

He fell silent. Sarah sighed and took his hand between hers.

"I'm gonna miss you. I don't suppose you're going to tell me how it's done? Thought not. I think I can figure it out though." She ran her thumb in small circles over his knucklebones. "I hearby release your vampiric powers." She paused to find the words. "Forever."

She half expected Grimalkin to return to that towering god of darkness he had been the other night, but instead he merely sighed.

"I'm sure the estate will allow you to leave. I...good luck, Grimalkin." She placed his hand on his chest and stood to leave, then paused as she heard him mutter in the dark.

"Berkleys. You're all alike. You work wonders until you decide to start following the *rules*."

Sarah waited a heartbeat in case he was going to say more, but he fell silent. He was probably trying to work out how to get around her restrictions, she thought.

She walked back upstairs, grabbing her keys with the intention of heading into Armstead for some food. She glanced at the portrait on her way out, but it hadn't changed. She wasn't too bothered--her instincts were telling her, from the point of view of becoming master of the manor, she was doing the right thing. When it came to the point of view of breaking her own heart she wasn't so sure. She fully expected the painting to change back by the time Grimalkin left the grounds.

She wanted to believe the best in him, that he would keep her trust, but she couldn't be sure, and part of her was steeling herself to hunt him down. She wouldn't bind him, she decided. If it came to that, then permanent death was kinder.

It was only when she was halfway through her breakfast that she remembered her cousin. She drove over to his house with the intention to gauge the extent of, and try to repair, any damage. To her surprise, his house was closed up and silent and no one answered her knocks. Maybe she'd frightened him away.

Somewhat relieved, and feeling too emotionally fragile to go back to the house, she went back to the library to start tidying up the loose ends of her previous life, and reassure her foster family that she hadn't dropped off the face of the earth.

Grimalkin had sensed her leave and not return, and he spent the rest of the day brooding. He hadn't considered the possibility that he was holding her back from her birthright, but the more he thought about it the more plausible it seemed.

But he was free. He couldn't help but smile at the thought. He could go anywhere, except near her, and do anything, except see her. She was just one person, he told himself; he had the entire night as compensation. He was free, and he could feel the bloodlust rising, chafing at the restrictions sunlight placed upon him.

He had made a vow to himself, so long ago he'd forgotten why, that he would always be happy. While he'd been bound in the dungeon, the vow, along with most of his mind, had been lost to the torture of endless thirst, but when he had been awakened he'd remembered it.

Thinking about Sarah *hurt*, and made him miserable, and so he would push her from his mind. He could hunt, he could feed, and he was going to be happy. And so he spent the rest of the day twitching impatiently, letting the beast have its head; the man he didn't want to think about.

When evening finally fell, Sarah still hadn't returned. Grimalkin, by this stage, couldn't have cared less. He guessed that she was getting out of the way for when he was going to leave. And a good thing, too, the beast snarled, he was strong and powerful and must feed, *must feed.*

He loped off, moving as fast as the night wind, causing small warm-blooded creatures to instinctively flinch and dart towards their burrows. Grimalkin ignored them; he was out for bigger prey, something that would beg for mercy.

Chapter 10

When Sarah returned to the house, she knew he was gone. The library had thrown her out around five, and she had had an early dinner at the café.

Some of her bravado had worn off, and she faced the empty house, and the future, with trepidation. The unlighted windows stared blindly at her and she suddenly felt very small.

No, she thought, *I don't need him to do this.* Sarah had a great desire to go to bed and hide under the covers, but she recognized the fact that if she did she'd feel worse. She had to do something proactive, even if it was just a tiny little thing, so that some of her self-confidence would hopefully return.

She picked her way across the potholes, half her mind on getting the driveway fixed and half on wondering where her family's papers actually were--she'd never got around to asking Grimalkin about them--when a tiny warning flag raised in her mind.

Sarah stopped and looked around, suddenly alert for any danger. All the sounds of the night were there, the owls in the woods and the wind in the trees and the creaking of the cast iron gate...

Sarah glanced back behind her, but the front gate was locked securely; unlike the Cox's, Sarah made a point of doing up all the locks. So where was the noise coming from? She couldn't suppress a shudder when she remembered that there was only one other iron gate on the property--the one to the family cemetery.

Her first instinct was to see if Grimalkin was playing games, but she squished that and headed quickly and quietly for the armory. Sarah slipped through the darkened house, the only illumination provided by the faint light from outside. The more she thought about it the less likely it seemed that this was Grimalkin's doing. Hiding in graveyards wasn't his style, she decided, and she didn't think he was capable of getting through the magical locks. But someone was. She remembered all too clearly that afternoon where the place had been searched--she assumed it had been Hegerty, but as her stomach clenched in fear, she wasn't so sure.

She grabbed the shotgun from before and filled her pockets with shells. She also took the Walther and stuck it in the waistband of her jeans--a terribly unsafe place to put it, but firearms safety wasn't her first priority at this point.

She loaded the shotgun without looking as she strode through the house; the gun primed with a satisfying 'chick-chunk'. Sarah slipped out the back door, her shoes making little sound on the short grass.

She couldn't help it; she wished Grimalkin was there. She felt exposed without the vampire guarding her back. *I'll guard my own back,* she thought fiercely, raising the barrels of her shotgun a fraction.

The garden looked even more eerie and dreamlike at night, with the moonlight turning the scene into a monochrome of silver and shadow. Sarah moved slowly and quietly, following the soul-scraping creak of cold iron and eventually she came within sight of the graveyard.

It was anticlimactic really. The gate was indeed swinging free on its hinges, but the scene appeared to be deserted. Sarah wasn't taking any chances, however, and she edged forward, her finger resting on the trigger guard.

Empty. The graveyard wasn't large, and Sarah could see from the gate that there was no one hiding there. And yet, it was emptier than it should have been. For one of the graves had been disturbed, and instead of grass and wildflowers was a huge, gaping hole.

Sarah felt real fear for the first time. The moonlight did little to penetrate the wounded earth, and Sarah felt vertiginous as she stared into the abyss; it appeared to be miles deep. She took a deep breath, and stepped out of the graveyard, leaving the gate untouched; it would make too much noise if she tried to shut it.

She crept around the side of the house, trying to keep to the shadows. Cautiously, she peered around the side of the building into the front yard. She squinted, trying to see into the shadows--was that movement? Just a plant nodding to itself in the night breeze.

She was about to go back the other way when she heard a soft shuffling sound from near the front steps. She waited, hardly daring to breath. It came again, strange footfalls, as if made by feet almost obscenely soft.

Sarah gripped the shotgun tighter. She couldn't hide forever--she had to defend her land. Screwing up her courage, she stepped quietly forward, her gaze and her gun trained on the front steps of her ancient house.

Her gaze was met.

Sarah had carefully crafted a mental picture of what she might see. After all, she had watched zombie films as a teenager and there were only a limited number of things that could come out of an occupied grave.

Nothing could have prepared her for what she saw pawing at her front door. For one thing, it was huge, at least eight feet tall and as fat as a grave-worm. Clothing hung in rags, stretched tight across rotting, waxy skin bloated by dark magic. Sarah couldn't see any ears, just holes in the side of its head.

Nevertheless, it heard her. There wasn't much left of its face; a swollen and distorted mockery of what once was a man. She recognized it anyway.

"Uncle." She spoke a single word to herself. This was the true monster in her family, a bitter mockery of her own flesh and blood, the rot that had eaten away at her life for so long. She didn't hesitate to pull the trigger.

Her weapon shredded the quiet of the night, sending the sleeping birds in the pines wheeling into the sky in fright. The projectiles thudded into the mound of flesh before her, causing it to shudder with the impact. It did not fall.

She fired again, and broke open the gun to reload, her movements jerky with just a tinge of panic. Again she fired, and again the monster kept on coming, absorbing both the lead and whatever magical enhancements her father had placed upon it.

Sarah swore and reloaded again. Why wasn't it working? *I'm not a magician,* she thought despairingly. *I don't know what's wrong.* Forcing herself to think logically, Sarah began to step sideways, trying to lure the abomination away from the front door. If this gun wasn't working there had to be something in the armory that would. Sarah thought longingly of the rocket launcher.

It wasn't until the thing that was her uncle suddenly changed tactics that Sarah realized there was more to this that she first thought. As if jerked on a string, the creature suddenly stumbled sideways, to keep itself between her and the door.

"It takes two to get out of the grave," Sarah ground out between clenched teeth. Rage flooded through her as she realized what a bad strategic position she was in. Between her and her weapons was not only the animated corpse of her hated uncle, but an unknown necromancer.

She had to get around the back, she realized; get through the house to the armory. The monster would have some trouble making it through the door, and she could hopefully take out the necromancer.

Sarah reloaded; she was running out of shells, and wasn't carrying any extra ammunition for the pistol digging into the small of her back. Taking a deep breath, she braced herself and *ran*.

She took off like a startled deer, her heart pounding in her chest. She didn't dare to imagine what would happen if her foot caught on a pothole. She could barely feel her feet hit the ground she was going so fast. She could see the corpse try to lumber after her, but its bulk slowed it down.

Sarah didn't hear the shot. She just felt the impact in her chest, knocking her sideways. She spun, pulling the trigger out of reflex as the shot scattered harmlessly against the side of the house. She hadn't time to brace herself for the impact with the ground, only to curse despairingly the beginner's luck that had brought down a target moving as fast as her.

Grimalkin was rather ruefully making plans. He had decided to get as far away from his ex-prison as possible, and had accordingly been loping beside the main road out of town for half an hour or so, keeping an eye out for a likely victim.

After coming across a herd of cattle, Grimalkin decided he had to get to a city as soon as possible; the countryside was practically deserted after dark. He wasn't the type to try and break into people's houses, although he'd been considering making an exception until he'd come across the unfortunate bovines. He'd only killed one, but it had spooked the others and they were now lowing unhappily from the opposite end of the field.

Of course, now that he was no longer half-mad with bloodlust he could reflect upon the lack of blonde-haired, steel-eyed lovers in his life. He wandered more slowly now, staring at his feet and concocting wild fantasies about bumping into Sarah at some unlikely location and convincing her that she couldn't live without him.

How likely was that? He snorted; he'd never managed to change her mind about anything before. And he had to face the fact; if he actually ever came face-to-face with her again he'd have enough trouble keeping himself under control. He reflected that it had been somewhat of a relief not to have to watch himself all the time, to have to second-guess the beast at every turn. Bah, he was just out of practice, he shook himself.

When he heard the faint reports from a shotgun echoing faintly through the night air from over the horizon he wasn't very surprised. He did wonder why the hunter hadn't been about earlier to provide a more satisfying hunt than cows, but merely shrugged and kept walking.

The next two shots made his ears prick up. What requires four shotgun blasts? No, six. He frowned and scented the air, although nothing but faint sound carried that distance. It sounded like whoever was shooting was barely taking time to reload before firing again.

It couldn't be. Surely it would take longer than that for her to get into trouble. He snarled contemptuously; if it was her, then she could look after herself. It was what she'd wanted after all.

He'd gone about three steps before he stopped again with a sigh. He couldn't do it; he couldn't turn his back on her. She had been trying so hard to do the right thing; it wasn't her fault she was probably trying too hard.

He was probably going to make a fool out of himself, he knew. He also knew he had no choice; the trappings may have been removed, but in some fundamental way he was still *hers*. He hoped she wouldn't take his interference the wrong way.

I'll be your guardian angel one more time, Sarah. Please forgive me for it.

Sarah hit the ground, the air knocked out of her lungs. Blood bloomed across her shirt from the wound in her side. She gasped for breath like a stranded fish, desperately hoping that her lung wasn't punctured and filling with blood. She braced herself for a second shot, but none came.

He was playing with her, she realized, and the thought spurred her into trying to get to her feet. She got to her knees, propping herself up with the shotgun. She stared at the house, trying to work out which of the windows her would-be assassin was lurking behind. She only allowed herself a few seconds--her uncle was still shuffling inexorably closer.

She staggered to her feet, ignoring the pain and the warm flow of blood from her wound. Her uncle was nearly upon her. No light of triumph sparked in those dead, rotting eyes, but Sarah knew there was no way she could win this fight. Her weapons, she realized as she raised the shotgun for the final time, were hopelessly inadequate.

She managed to get off a shot before one of the abomination's massive hands swiped down, and with obscene strength, tore the weapon from her hands. Sarah stumbled back a few steps, reaching around to pull out the pistol. The weapon felt ludicrously small. Bracing herself, Sarah took careful aim, and put a bullet through her uncle's left eye--or what remained of it.

It had been her last hope and, when the creature paused, her heart leaped. It stopped and gave a strange little shake, and then stepped forward again. Sarah felt tears of hopelessness prick at her eyes; she had been so sure of herself, she'd felt so strong. It can't end like this, she thought despairingly as the rotting bulk loomed up in front of her.

Sarah felt more than saw the force that approached so impossibly fast. There was a weird echoing yowl and a sense of mass fast approaching--and then something slammed into the animated corpse with the power of a runaway train.

Sarah blinked, trying to work out just what the huge shadowy thing that attached itself to the creature was. Her uncle backhanded the thing, throwing it off; heedless of the flesh it tore. It landed on its feet a couple yards away from the corpse and let loose another eerie roar.

Sarah felt she had fallen down the rabbit hole; all sense of normal scale vanished. Her savior was a grey cat, about the same proportions as an ordinary housecat. And about fifty times the size.

In the split second that Sarah got a clear glimpse of it, she saw it was about the size of a pony, its head roughly level with her collarbone. When it roared, it revealed teeth about half a foot long, and for a moment its eyes met hers. Red eyes.

"Grim," she whispered.

There was no acknowledgement from the cat. The feline sprang at her uncle, claws and teeth tearing at the fat, white flesh. Her uncle met it with a punch that caused it to snarl in pain. Sarah decided that Grimalkin had this battle well in hand, and she turned her gaze to the house.

"Thank you," she called over her shoulder, as she started stalking purposefully towards the front door. Her blood had clotted into an uncomfortable sticky mess on her side, but the pain had receded enough for her to believe she was in no danger from the wound. She reflected that the bullet had probably hit a rib, cracking the bone but leaving her internal organs intact.

Let our subordinates fight it out, she thought grimly. *This is between you and me.* She had a fair idea who was lurking in her house--only another Berkley could have breached the family defenses so easily.

Sarah kicked open the front door, sweeping the room with her pistol. She glanced briefly at the portrait and gasped; all the colors were running together, leaving only the vaguest suggestion of what was painted on there previously. *So the succession is still up in the air,* she thought. The place must be wide open; it was no wonder Grimalkin hadn't had any trouble getting back in.

She padded forward, her finger on the trigger. Where would he be waiting for her? She lowered the gun and closed her eyes, letting her instinct guide her. He was...at the same place he'd been last time; the grand dining hall where his employees had impaled Grimalkin what seemed like a century ago.

Sarah strode forward and applied her foot to the carved wooden door. It flew open with a bang, surprising the only occupant. John Berkley turned around to find himself staring down the barrel of Sarah's pistol.

He didn't seem overly surprised to see her. He had a book in his hands, and Sarah notice a rifle propped up against the wall out of the corner of her eye. He didn't make a move for it.

"The vampire is back," he said, looking worried. "We have to work together on this, it's the only way."

"Only way to do what? As far as I'm concerned, if he makes himself useful he can stay as long as he likes."

"Sarah, he's *unbound.* You've seen how powerful he is--he'll kill us both."

"My house; my problem. Not yours, my dearest cousin."

"Are you planning on killing me?"

"Think of it as returning the favor," Sarah spat.

"I wasn't going to kill you. Not intentionally, I just wanted you to give up your right to the collection."

"You resurrected your own *father* as a corpse!"

"I thought it was somewhat fitting, considering how he died."

"And how did he die?" Sarah asked, although even as she said the words she had the horrible feeling that somehow she already knew.

John stared at her for a moment and then said with incredulous anger. "Why, you killed him."

Sarah opened her mouth to refute this allegation but the words died on her lips. A final memory, hiding behind all the others, of a little girl prying a gun from the fingers of a dead man surfaced in her mind. Of the vampire killing all but her uncle and the man she later knew as Hegerty. Hegerty ran, her uncle didn't.

"He was trying to kill a twelve year old girl. I'd say I was justified."

Justified in raising the pistol, as the vampire, now apparently about twelve years old, grinned madly, watching the man look at her with real fear in his eyes, hearing him beg. And pulling the trigger, being surprised at how it jumped in her hands, and watching a man die, with a monster murmuring praise in her ear.

"He was my *father!*" her cousin cried.

"Oh, please, don't try and pretend this was for revenge. Maybe it was once, but that book in your hands tells me you care more about the collection now. There is no justification for what you or your father did."

"If you kill me now you'll be just as dead when the vampire finishes fighting out there."

"I don't think he's really a vampire," Sarah said thoughtfully. "I think *he* thinks he is."

"What?"

"Do you have any last words?" Sarah asked.

"As a matter of fact I do," John snarled. "*Declaratio mearcian-*"

He got no further. Sarah pulled the trigger, and a neat little hole appeared right between John's eyes. He didn't make a sound until his lifeless body hit the wooden floor.

Sarah gave a sad sigh of relief and finally lowered the pistol. Her arms were killing her, and if she hadn't spent all those years practicing, in her exhausted state she wouldn't have been able to hit a thing. Still, things were far from over.

She cocked her head and listened. The faint sounds of combat from outside had ceased, and she had no doubt as to who the winner was. At least his name makes sense now, she thought. She was taking a big risk, waiting for him armed with only a half-empty pistol, and she was aware that she was still covered in her own blood. Nevertheless, she stood over the corpse of her nearest relative and waited.

She heard him enter the front door, walking on two legs instead of four again. His true form had come as quite a surprise, and she was still trying to work out what it meant.

He pushed open the other half of the double doors to the room and just stood here, regarding her with eyes like garnets. She could feel it, just has she had before, that aura of power, the essence of the night itself that wrapped itself lovingly around him. Like a mother's embrace--the odd thought floated across her consciousness.

"Thank you, Grimalkin. I think it's over now." She did not allow herself to be overwhelmed by his presence again; she could feel the patterns of power here shifting. Somehow the house was becoming hers, and it gave her a strange source of strength.

He didn't say anything; he just took a step forward. She raised her gun.

"Sarah," he said softly. Their eyes met over the sights of the gun and they just watched each other for a few heartbeats. Eventually Sarah gave a strange little smile and lowered her gun. It was time to see if her gamble had paid off, and the stakes couldn't have been higher.

He stepped forward again, not stopping until he was close enough for her to see the stitching on his coat. He smiled again, the points of his fangs grazing his lower lip.

Sarah tilted her head up as she felt his fingers slide along her neck and graze her jawbone. She watched his eyes dance as he examined her face, and then she watched them close. His hand slid around the nape of her neck and up to tangle his fingers in her hair. He bent his head and pressed his lips to hers.

Sarah had to admit, it was scary. She could feel his fangs against the sensitive skin of her lips, and she knew there was no safety net. Despite the danger, her heart sang and she raised her hand to caress his cheek.

"Grim," she whispered against his lips when they finally broke apart.

"I did it," he said, somewhat thickly.

"I knew you could." She looked about. "We've got some cleaning up to do."

"No wait, there's still more," he said. Sarah's eyes widened in surprise as he got down on his knees. His eyes were level with the bloodstain on her shirt, and he had to shake his head to clear it.

"Grimalkin, what are you doing?"

"I hereby bind my vampiric powers to Sarah Berkley, to be at her command, to protect her, for as long as she remains in this world."

"Grim, I-"

"Do you accept?" he asked, almost pleading.

"I...y-yes."

He stood and smiled at her. "Now we can clean up. And you need medical attention--preferably from someone better trained than I."

"But why, Grim?"

"Well, it's probably not that bad, but I think you'll need stitches."

"No, I mean," she looked up at him, "why did you come back?"

"Because I love you," he said simply, "even if you don't love me back."

"Grim, I couldn't-"

"I know. I was pretty hard on you. Although if I recall you gave as good as you got. The fact that you still want me around is enough."

"Can we discuss this later? Although I will say now," she walked over and put her arm around him, "I really didn't want to let you go. But I felt even worse about locking you up."

"I can't complain now," he grinned, wrapping his arm across her shoulders. "Everything I get I brought on myself."

"And boy are you gonna get it."

"I am?" He looked down at her in surprise.

"Oh, yeah, in every room of the house."

"But...argh." Sarah laughed at the flustered look on his face. "That's inappropriate talk for someone who's supposed to be injured."

"You know what?"

"What?"

"I think I do love you, Grimalkin. It's just going to take some getting used to the idea." She thought that if he didn't stop grinning he was going to give himself a jaw ache.

Grimalkin picked up the remains of her cousin and slung them unceremoniously over his shoulder. Sarah wandered out ahead of him to examine the portrait.

"Hey, Grim, come and have a look at this."

He wandered out to see his master face to face with her painted double, which stared imperiously down from the canvas, the magically rendered gaze suggesting hidden knowledge.

"Congratulations," he said.

"No, you're here, too. Come and see."

The painted figure had a gun tucked into her belt, but her hands were free to hold a coil of leather, the other end of which was attached to the collar of a small, grey cat with red eyes, sitting at her feet.

"It's so cute," Sarah laughed.

"It's not to scale," Grimalkin replied sourly.

"If it was to scale you wouldn't fit into the painting. Just be happy you're there at all."

"Oh, I am, Master, more than I can say."

If I'm in the painting that means I'm going to be with you for as long as you're the Master of the Hunt. Maybe you will let me extend your life to match mine, and maybe you won't. But either way, I will be your devoted servant until the end of time.

You can find ALL our books up at on our website at:

http://www.writers-exchange.com

All our romances:

http://www.writers-exchange.com/category/genres/romance/

all our fantasy novels:

http://www.writers-exchange.com/category/genres/fantasy/

About the Author

Lorienne hails from country Queensland, Australia, and grew up among gum trees and soybean crops as well as horses, cats and many kinds of creepy-crawlies.

She was first published at the age of six in the school magazine and has been writing ever since.

In 2005 she graduated with both a Bachelor of Arts and a Bachelor of Science, majoring in Mathematics and Philosophy.

She currently lives in Brisbane in a big share-house with five of her closest friends.

You can keep track of Lorienne's books on her author page: http://www.writers-exchange.com/Lorienne-Walk/

If you enjoyed this author's book, then please place a review up at the site of purchase and any social media sites you frequent!